To love

The minister's gaze focused on Nikki; she had the vague impression that he had asked her if she would promise to love and honor the man who stood beside her.

She nodded, feeling voiceless. Gil squeezed her hand. "I do," she finally managed to say. Somewhere a peacock screamed, and another shrieked in answer.

Nikki watched as Gil slipped a lovely band of platinum and diamonds onto her finger. Then Loretta was tugging at her sleeve and offering Nikki another platinum ring—a man's. Numbly Nikki took it and slid it over Gil's knuckle and securely onto his finger.

The minister pronounced them husband and wife. Nikki sucked in her breath sharply.

Gil drew the veil back from her face. "Nikki," he said, his voice low and strained, "there's only one thing wrong with this wedding. It isn't real."

Dear Reader,

Our wedding was small and took place before a judge in the courthouse. Our honeymoon was modest, one day and one night—all we could spare.

But our wedding journey—now *that* was something. We were merging two households of pets into one, and moving from Illinois to Arkansas, a journey of some five hundred miles. The supporting cast of this exodus was as follows:

Sophie—a dachshund	Sir Isaac—an adventurous newt
Mollie—a terrier	Fig—Isaac's evil twin
Snoopy—a white cat	Fang—a fighting fish
Willie—son of Snoopy	Edgar—a guinea pig
Esther—a snapping turtle	Sir Hiss—an amiable serpent
Wart—Esther's consort	Golum—a large iguana

We were going to transport this menagerie to Arkansas by car. We would also tow a trailer containing forty boxes of books and an upright piano.

Reader, imagine it is the first week of your marriage. You are caught in St. Louis rush-hour traffic with twelve animals and your piano. Your new husband is coming down with food poisoning, and somehow your newts have gotten loose in the car.

My husband and I looked at each other (across two cats and an iguana) and figured if we made it through *this*, we should be able to make it through anything.

Well, we did. We got to Arkansas, all fourteen of us, although the newts were a bit the worse for wear. And, as for my husband and me, I'm glad to say we'd do it again!

Sincerely,

Bethany Campbell

ONLY
MAKE-BELIEVE
Bethany Campbell

Harlequin Books

TORONTO • NEW YORK • LONDON
AMSTERDAM • PARIS • SYDNEY • HAMBURG
STOCKHOLM • ATHENS • TOKYO • MILAN
MADRID • WARSAW • BUDAPEST • AUCKLAND

ISBN 0-373-03230-7

Harlequin Romance first edition November 1992

ONLY MAKE-BELIEVE

Printed in U.S.A.

CHAPTER ONE

THE MAN WHO'D COME backstage seemed a strange sort. He reminded Nikki of an ill-tempered, wizened elf incongruously dressed as a Manhattan businessman. Despite his size, he exuded an air of wealth and self-importance.

Normally, Nikki would not have let him into her dressing room. But Evelyn, who was part owner of the nightclub, had escorted him herself, and Evelyn was ferociously protective of all her performers. Nevertheless, Evelyn's face was troubled.

In a small, creaking voice, the man announced that he was a lawyer by the name of Laslow Roach. Nikki, seated at her dressing table, was still in full makeup and costume. Without waiting to be asked, Roach commandeered the room's only other chair, perching on its edge. The polished tips of his expensive shoes just touched the floor.

Imperiously he told Evelyn to leave the dressing room so he could talk to Nikki. Surprisingly, Evelyn complied. She whirred off in her wheelchair, chain-smoking as usual, a concerned expression remaining on her face.

Nikki was puzzled, but she had guessed three things about the tiny man. First, he was rich; second, he was humorless; and third, whatever he thought about her he was, in all probability, wrong. Appearances, especially Nikki's, could be deceiving. She was a young woman with secrets, and she kept them well.

At the moment, Nikki looked wealthy and beautiful, swathed in diamonds, a woman for whom great things lay in store. In reality, the diamonds were fake, she had a complicated past, and all she really wanted was a simple future. She never entertained thoughts of attaining greatness. She knew better.

But Nikki wondered what a lawyer could want with her. Evelyn wouldn't have let him backstage unless she thought him completely respectable. The older woman had promised to watch out for Nikki, and she did so with a vengeance.

Laslow Roach was perhaps fifty years old, shorter and slighter than Nikki, yet somehow forbidding. He wore an expensive overcoat of cashmere, and he did not take it off. Although he looked far too warm in the crowded dressing room, his eyes, when he gazed at Nikki, were cold.

His small, scratchy voice was equally cold. "I have a proposition for you. Strictly legitimate. I can make your biggest dream come true. I mean it. Your biggest."

What kind of corny line was that? Nikki wondered. *Why on earth did Evelyn bring him here? Was she slipping?*

Nikki gave Roach a cool smile and shook her head. Whatever he wanted, he couldn't have approached her in a worse way.

Nikki Tripp had seen too often what big dreams did to people. Her dreams were small, and she planned to keep them so. It was, she believed, the only safe way to live.

For years she and her aunt, Rhonda, had existed on the less respectable fringes of show business, and it was the only life that Nikki knew. Rhonda, in her haphazard way, had loved it. Nikki hadn't loved it then and didn't now.

All her life, Rhonda had aspired to be somebody. Nikki's most burning ambition was to be nobody except herself—and nothing except ordinary.

Her present life was far from ordinary. Six nights a week she made her living by pretending to be various rich and famous somebodies who'd made something of themselves.

As Rhonda before her, Nikki was a professional impersonator in Evelyn's Greenwich Village nightclub. It was a club that missed being seedy by the barest of margins.

After Rhonda's death, Evelyn, with her bulldog disposition, took it upon herself to protect Nikki. How had Laslow Roach slipped past Evelyn's usually fierce guard?

Nikki turned her attention from Roach to her mirror. He watched her with the same disquieting coldness. She was unclasping her rhinestone necklace when he spoke again.

"I want you to go to Las Vegas. Pretend to be Caressa. Get married."

He did not so much as blink as he stated the proposition. Then, taking a gold case from his overcoat, he handed her an engraved card. She was too rattled to do more than glance at it.

"I'm Caressa's chief legal representative," he said.

"What?" Nikki demanded, astonished.

"I want you to go to Vegas. Impersonate Caressa. Get married."

His words hardly registered. Instead Nikki heard the ghost of her aunt's husky, ruined voice. It came back, haunting her with Rhonda's old will-o'-the-wisp fantasies: *Oh, Nikki, life's a merry-go-round and everybody tries to grab the gold ring. If it ever comes in reach, you have to grab for it. Who knows? You just might grab your heart's desire.*

Nikki's skin prickled. She didn't know whether to take the spectral voice as an omen of encouragement or one of warning. So she simply stared at Roach, pretending she felt nothing more than amused skepticism.

Roach stared back, his gray eyes hard. He shifted so that the toes of his shoes touched the floor more firmly. Flushed with heat and impatience, he awaited her answer.

Nikki's answer was a laugh. Her laugh was a croaky chuckle, at odds with her perfect makeup and the silver

spangles of her gown. When threatened, she often retreated into aloofness and flippancy, and she did so now.
"This is ridiculous," she said. "You're making this up."

No smile crossed Roach's withered face. "No. It's real.
This is a security matter, and Caressa's security people want
you in Vegas, to pretend you're her, to get married."

"Married?" Nikki laughed again. "Pretend I'm Caressa
and get *married?* What's the matter? Is she making so much
money she can't take the time to do it herself?"

Roach must be the victim of some mad delusion, she
thought. Oh, she could imitate Caressa, all right. Ruefully
she looked at herself in the mirror. She *did* look eerily like
the star, but only because it was her job to do so.

She still had on her Caressa costume, the elaborate
makeup, and her hair remained in the crimped cascade that
Caressa had made famous. There were over two thousand
silver sequins on her form-fitting dress. She knew because
she had sewn on every cursed one of them.

"Not *really* married, of course." Roach's tone was impatient. "Don't laugh. This is serious. Caressa has the best
security people, and they've put *thought* into this. You pretend to get married. You lead the press astray, away from
her. You're a decoy."

A decoy, Nikki thought facetiously. She imagined a duck
decoy, floating among the reeds. For her added amusement, she put a blond wig on its head. "And who am I supposed to *pretend* to marry? Gavin Chandler—like the gossip
columnists say?"

"Precisely," the little lawyer said without smiling. Nikki
laughed again. Gavin Chandler, the film star, was as famous as Caressa.

A tall, blue-eyed actor from Australia, he had achieved
almost instant stardom in the States. One magazine had
immediately dubbed him the sexiest man in the world.

"Right," Nikki said with irony. "I marry Gavin Chandler. All in a day's work."

She shook her head. Evelyn must have let Roach backstage as a joke, just so she and Nikki could laugh about it later. Although Roach had an aura of cold-blooded sanity, what he said was sheer madness.

"Not Gavin Chandler," he said testily. "Caressa does that. In private. Far from Vegas. Your job is to be seen with somebody who passes for Chandler. Play kissy face. Buy a license. Have a ceremony. Make it look real. Draw attention away from her and Chandler."

Nikki gave him a cool smile. "Pass for Chandler? He's Adonis. Nobody can pass for him."

Roach's face stayed stony. "This guy's done it. And he can do it again—from a distance. He's his double, a stuntman."

"A stuntman," Nikki said, rolling her eyes with mockery. "This gets better and better."

Roach ignored her facetiousness. "It's simple—you two act as decoys. You keep the press distracted, away from Caressa and Chandler. You don't let yourself be seen up close—just a glimpse here, a glimpse there. Hide-and-seek with the paparazzi—drive them crazy. Over Thanksgiving, while she and Chandler get married. All your expenses paid—you'll live like a queen. *And* we pay you a salary of ten thousand dollars."

The smile on Nikki's face swiftly vanished. Had he actually said *ten thousand dollars?*

A dizzy, sick feeling struck the pit of her stomach, and she picked up his card and studied it. The words that danced before her eyes made her dizzier still.

Suddenly Nikki understood why Evelyn had let him backstage. He had the power to offer an enormous sum of money—an unbelievable sum—*ten thousand dollars.*

"Not so flip, now, are you?" Roach asked, almost maliciously. "Money talks, right?"

Stunned, Nikki turned to her mirror. "Maybe it does," she said, acting calmer than she felt. "Maybe it doesn't." She took off her glittering earrings.

"I've explained it all to your manager," Roach said, watching her with predatory concentration. "She understands this is legitimate—and very lucrative. She—approves."

Nikki nodded mechanically. Evelyn wasn't exactly her manager, but she'd watched out for Nikki since Rhonda's death. No wonder the expression on Evelyn's face had been so odd. She had known what Roach was going to say.

Under the rhinestones and silver sequins of Nikki's gown, her heart beat crazily. Ten thousand dollars could get her out of show business. Ten thousand dollars could open the door to a new life for her—even a new one for Evelyn, if Evelyn, stubborn as she was, would ever agree.

Ten thousand dollars—it was a fortune, but Caressa could afford it. Caressa made millions of dollars. In the last ten years, she had become a legend.

Caressa's face stared from half the magazines on the newsstands. The tabloids incessantly screamed her name, yet could not seem to get enough of her. She had become the first bona fide blond goddess since Marilyn Monroe.

"Caressa picked you herself," Roach said. "From pictures. This'll give your career a big shot in the arm. You should be honored."

Nikki brushed the crimping out of her blond hair, allowing it to fall to its natural straightness. She knew that she shouldn't appear too eager; for one thing, the proposition was far too strange.

"I don't intend to make *this* my career," she said. She made a dismissive shrug. She gave her hair a few finishing strokes, pulled it back and fastened it into place with a barrette. She was blond and blue-eyed, like Caressa, but without the makeup and costume, the resemblance vanished. Nikki's real features were pretty rather than dramatic, almost delicate.

For three years, since she was eighteen and Rhonda was dying, Nikki had earned her way by being an impersonator in this nightclub, so aptly named Mirages. All the club's performers imitated famous people—Elvis Presley, Barbra Streisand, Michael Jackson, Diana Ross, Janet Jackson. Nikki had learned her specialities by watching Rhonda, who had imitated both Caressa and Marilyn Monroe.

She disliked the job, but knew she was lucky Evelyn had let her have it. It paid better than any other work she would have found, and Nikki was saving her money. She had plans.

"I'm asking for less than a week of your time," Roach said. His eyes seemed as dispassionate as a reptile's. "Think about it. How long would it take to make ten thousand dollars—clear—working in this firetrap?"

Nikki shrugged again, feigning indifference. The money sounded unbelievable, but suddenly she wasn't sure she wanted to try to fool the world in earnest. The idea sounded bizarre, even frightening.

"Look," she said with false carelessness, "do you think it's fun pretending to be somebody else? Especially Caressa? She's *very* difficult to bring off. I can do it on the stage—when the audience knows it's an illusion. But in real life? Twenty-four hours a day? You don't know what you're asking."

Roach gave a diminutive snort. "No, *you* look. This is a plum assignment. You fly to Las Vegas in Caressa's private jet. You get to wear her mink coats. You even get to wear duplicates of her jewelry."

"Wow," Nikki said, taking off her cheap bracelets. "Duplicates of her jewelry. Wow. I guess somebody like me couldn't be trusted with the real thing."

Roach scowled. "Don't be mouthy. Even Caressa doesn't wear the real stuff. It's too *expensive* to wear. It's too expensive to have anywhere except in a vault."

Nikki took refuge in irreverence again. "How the rich and famous do suffer."

She turned to the mirror. She draped a towel around her shoulders and began to pat on cold cream to help take off her makeup. She would have gladly changed her clothes first, but with Roach sitting there, she had no place to do so.

Nikki decided to keep on her false eyelashes and eyeliner for the time being. She didn't like anyone seeing her completely devoid of makeup. The eyelashes were a safety barrier she could keep between herself and Roach.

"The rich and famous *do* suffer," Roach said. His small body swelled with rectitude. "They suffer from lack of privacy. Caressa wants to get married. She doesn't want this marriage to be a media circus—"

Like her last one? Nikki thought wryly. But she knew better than to say it.

Roach perched more precariously on the edge of the chair. "Marriage is sacred," he said, sounding more righteous every moment. "The media will try to exploit this very *sacred,* this very *personal,* very *private* moment of Caressa's. She's a human being, like you and me. She wants to be married in her parents' home—quietly—with her own family around her. At Thanksgiving. The press has *got* to be drawn away. I'm offering you a chance to help another human being—*and* make ten thousand dollars."

Nikki forced her breathing to stay steady and kept her expression stubbornly blank. Should she do it? More frighteningly, was she *capable* of doing it?

"Ten thousand is a king's ransom," Roach grumbled. "And what's Thanksgiving? You've got no family. None to speak of. I know. I checked with your manager. It's not as if you'll miss dinner at Grandma's house with all the clan."

Nikki stiffened and her hand tightened around the tissue. She paused, then wiped away another streak of cold cream. "What did she say about my family?" she asked tightly.

"That you didn't have any."

Nikki swallowed and cleaned away the last of her makeup except around her eyes. The eyes, fringed with false lashes, looked out of place in her faintly freckled face. On close inspection, she looked far too young to pass for Caressa. She was twenty-one, fully thirteen years younger.

"You've got nobody," Roach said with unkind frankness. He looked around the dingy dressing room with mixed derision and disgust. "Not much to be thankful for, if you ask me."

"I didn't ask you." Nervously, she reached for a bottle of cleanser and started to remove the film of cold cream.

It was true that she had no family since Rhonda's death. Her only home was her apartment, two cramped rooms above the nightclub, upstairs from Evelyn.

As for Thanksgiving, it meant nothing to Nikki, nothing except pain and emptiness. Rhonda had died during the Thanksgiving season, and Evelyn, who disliked all holidays, never celebrated any of them.

"So why resist?" Roach prodded. "You'll never get another Thanksgiving like this. We're talking about the penthouse of the Xanadu Hotel, the lap of luxury. You should be paying *me* to do this, not the other way around."

Nikki swept her used tissues into a battered wastebasket. The longer she considered Roach's proposal, the more it unnerved her. Roach seemed like some strange imp who had appeared to bargain for her soul.

"I don't know," she said. "I'd lose work time here. I'd lose salary. I could put my job in danger. Evelyn isn't the only owner. I've got to keep other people happy, too."

"I've talked to Evelyn," Roach said. He put a cigarillo in his mouth and spoke around it. "I'll talk to everyone concerned. I *personally* guarantee your job will be safe. I'll personally see that you don't lose a dime. Caressa is a powerful woman. I can therefore *guarantee* these things. Besides, you can name where you want to work after this—better places than this fleabag."

Nikki pretended to be unimpressed, but a musing look crossed her face. She always had to keep money in mind, of course. She had promises to keep. But Roach's offer truly boggled her mind.

He lit his cigarillo, then squinted at her reflection in the mirror. "You know," he said with distaste, "without her cockamamy hairdo and makeup, you look eight years old. Except in the eyes. In the eyes you look about a hundred. No wonder you can play *her*."

"I have no desire to live with a *stuntman* over Thanksgiving," Nikki said stubbornly, taking off her scarlet nail polish. "Stuntmen aren't sane. They throw themselves off cliffs and walk through fire. I'd rather stay home."

Roach sighed with an unpleasant hiss. "Kid," he said, pointing a finger at her image in the mirror, "you're trying my patience. There's a hundred other impersonators in this town I could ask. What's the matter? Are you scared?"

Nikki kept her face expressionless and drew a deep breath. With all her heart she didn't want Roach to walk out of the room, taking away his offer and leaving only his cigarillo smoke behind. People said that money wasn't the answer to problems, but they didn't know. It could answer an enormous number of problems. It could answer hers.

Once more she heard Rhonda's echoing voice. *If the gold ring comes in reach, you have to grab for it. Who knows? You just might grab your heart's desire.*

But the suspicious part of Nikki's mind kept her apprehensive. "It could be dangerous," she said, no longer smiling. "Some of Caressa's fans are rabid. I know she gets threats. There are people out there who don't want her and Gavin Chandler to get married, some strange, *jealous* people who might try to stop it."

Roach made an impatient gesture, as if shooing away an insignificant fly. "So she gets threats—big deal. Everybody famous gets threats. You'll be in virtually no danger. Security will be maximum. You'll have absolutely the finest protection possible."

"No," Nikki said, more soberly than before. "I'd have the *second* best protection possible—*she'll* have the best. Celebrity weddings bring out the worst in people."

"Which is exactly why we need you," Roach said smoothly. "I'll tell you what. You're nervous? Money's a wonderful cure for nerves. I'll offer you *twelve* thousand dollars. And that is my absolute final offer, that's it, the end."

Twelve thousand, Nikki thought, blood racing. It was an almost impossible amount to imagine.

What, really, did she have to fear from some crazed fan of Caressa's or Chandler's? She wasn't a hothouse flower; she could take care of herself. Toward the end, she'd supported both herself and Rhonda, hadn't she? She needed more formal education, true; but she had street smarts.

And Roach was right: to impersonate Caressa, she'd need real security people around her—to make the charade convincing. She'd probably be safer in Vegas pretending to be Caressa than she was in New York as her humble self.

It was a minimal risk and a maximum reward—the money to start a new kind of life, a better one. *You just might grab your heart's desire.*

She swallowed. Then, meeting Roach's glittering eyes in the mirror, she gave him a businesslike nod. "Twelve thousand," she agreed, her heart leaping wildly.

His face stolid, he reached into his inside pocket and withdrew a sheaf of papers. "I've got an agreement here," he rasped. "I'll fill in the amount, you sign. Needless to say, confidentiality is of the essence. You and your manager mention this to nobody. Nobody—or the deal's off, void."

Nikki blanched at all the fine print on the contract. Her heart raced maniacally. "I'm not going to sign anything right *now.* Not without—without looking it over."

Roach scowled. "So look it over. I'll wait." He folded his arms.

Nikki hesitated. "No," she said at last with surprising firmness. "I'd feel rushed—with you looking over my shoulder. I—contracts are tricky. I want to understand every word. And I want Evelyn to see it, too."

He shrugged irritably. "All right, all right. Take it home tonight. But I mean it—absolute confidentiality. If this leaks to the press, there'll be repercussions. You'll pay, believe me—both of you. Believe me, Caressa has the power to *make* you pay."

"You don't have to threaten us," Nikki said with a cool smile. "We're harmless." But as the reality of her situation sank in, she no longer felt cool or flippant.

"You can have until tomorrow noon," Roach muttered with ill humor. "You know the southern fried chicken restaurant just around the corner from Radio City Music Hall?"

Nikki nodded.

"Stand outside. I'll pick you up there." He unfolded the contract, uncapped his fountain pen and, balancing the papers on his thigh, began to ink in the amount.

Twelve thousand dollars, Nikki thought dazedly. He was handing her the keys to the future of which she'd dreamed. In spite of her apprehension, her mind spun pleasantly, and her blood brightened in her veins. *Twelve thousand dollars.*

Roach rose and moved to Nikki's dressing table, setting the papers down before her.

"You'll be crazy if you don't sign, kid," he said in his hissing voice. "You go to Vegas free. For five days, you live like a goddess. *And* become the bride of Adonis."

Giddy, Nikki stared at the print on the contract without seeing it. *Twelve thousand dollars. A fortune.*

She tried to ignore the ominous knot tightening in her stomach. She did what she usually did when she was nervous. She hid her real emotions and laughed. "Too bad," she said, "it's only make-believe."

CHAPTER TWO

THE LIGHT OF A NEON SIGN fell spasmodically between the slats of the window blind. Neither Nikki or Evelyn noticed. They were used to the sign flashing all night long.

"I'm worried about this stuntman," Evelyn said. She squinted at Nikki through the cigarette smoke. "I mean it sounds like you're gonna have to *live* with him."

"I wish you'd quite smoking," Nikki said. "It's not good for you. Forget the stuntman. I can handle him. I grew up here, didn't I?"

She nodded toward the thin wall separating them from the club. Evelyn lived in a tiny apartment adjoining Mirages. Nikki lived in an even tinier one above it.

"Ha!" scoffed Evelyn, then coughed. "If you've got the same luck with men that Rhonda and I had, then you'd—"

"*—better just stay away from them.*" Nikki finished the sentence in chorus with Evelyn. She knew the warning by heart. It had rung through the last six years of her life like a mantra, endlessly repeated.

"You don't have to tell me," Nikki said. "I'm not like Rhonda. I don't want some man to take care of me. I want to take care of myself."

"Amen," Evelyn said with fierce conviction. She guided her chair to the kitchen counter and poured herself a cup of coffee. "*Always* to be able to take care of yourself," Evelyn said, wheeling back to the table. "That's the best advice I could give anybody. That—and stay out of show business. I wish somebody'd told *me*. Lord, do I wish it."

Evelyn shook her graying head ruefully. She was a round, hunched little woman with a seamed face and a bulldog's stubborn jaw. For all of her talk of taking care of oneself, she was not well, and Nikki worried about her. A bout of phlebitis had put her temporarily in the wheelchair, and the doctor kept cautioning her to rest. Evelyn never rested. She didn't know how.

Nikki leaned her elbow on the table. "With twelve thousand dollars, I could take care of myself, all right. I could finish school, pay for my training and everything. Move to Jersey and support myself while I learn the job. You could stop worrying about me. You could sell your share in the club and retire."

Evelyn glowered. "I don't keep my share of this club for *you.* I keep it because I can't find anybody *stupid* enough to buy it. I've told you a thousand times—you're on your own. You want advice from me? Fine. But I'm not responsible for you—*you're* responsible for you. I don't take care of you. *You* take care of you." She raised her chin pugnaciously, her tired eyes flashing with anger.

"I know, I know, I know," Nikki said, shrugging impatiently. But she wasn't fooled. She feared that Evelyn would never break free from the club's demands until Nikki was safely settled. The best way Nikki could repay the older woman's kindness was to make her own way. But that would take money.

"Look," Nikki said, trying a different tack. "You said the contract looks straightforward. No loopholes. That it's on the up-and-up."

Evelyn's face grew grimmer. "What do I know? I'm no lawyer. This *stuntman* worries me. Go off and live with a stuntman for five days? Mother-of-pearl!"

Nikki sat straighter, trying to look dignified and responsible. "Don't worry about the stuntman. What would I want with him? He's probably covered with alligator bites and old arrow wounds. Besides, what would he want with me?"

"Ha," snorted Evelyn. "Do you ever *really* look in a mirror? Except to paint over that pretty face? You're a beautiful young woman. What would he want? Ha! What do they *all* want?"

Impatience flooded Nikki's heart. "He won't get anything from *me.* I saw the mess Rhonda made out of her life over men—"

"Men *and* show business," Evelyn said in her tobacco-raspy voice. "A terrible combination. And what's a stunt-man? Nothing but a man *in* show business. And the worst kind—macho, reckless. These guys make money, you know. I don't want you finding him *glamorous* or something."

"Please!" Nikki said. "Stop obsessing—he's the least of my worries. The big thing is—can I do it? Be convincing? I mean it's twelve *thousand* dollars. Enough to buy a whole future. So can I do it?"

Evelyn studied Nikki through the smoke. Her cynical eyes looked more weary than before.

She's getting old, Nikki thought with sorrow. *She's sick, and she's tired and won't admit it. If I were on my own, she could get out of here, stop worrying, get well.*

"Well," she persisted, wanting Evelyn's faith, her encouragement, "what do you think? Can I do it?"

Evelyn looked more tired and pessimistic than before. She took a long drag from her cigarette. "Kid, it's a risky proposition—strange. It won't be—comfortable. I can't tell you what to do. You've got to make up your own mind."

Nikki shifted nervously. She had hoped for stronger support. Yet she felt as if Evelyn was sending her a mixed message.

Don't go. It could be bad for you—I worry.

Do go. It may be your only chance. I won't be around forever to watch out for you—I worry.

"I'm going to do it," Nikki said with a confidence she didn't feel. "What the heck—what can I lose?"

Misgiving shone out of Evelyn's eyes. "It's your choice," she said. "You're the one—" She began to cough.

Nikki rose to go to her, but impatiently Evelyn waved her back. "Just—get me—a drink," she said between coughs.

Nikki went to the sink, inwardly flinching at each asthmatic bark. She bit her lip as she ran the water, remembering how the doctor had warned Evelyn. If she didn't want emphysema, she should stop smoking. And if she didn't want another attack of phlebitis, she should stop worrying and working so hard.

But Evelyn kept on smoking and worrying and working as if she could never wear out. She stopped coughing at last, but tears of pain glinted in her eyes.

"As I was saying," Evelyn muttered, clutching the water glass, "it's your choice, kid."

No, Nikki thought. *It's not my choice. I've got to do this. For me. But for you, too.*

Evelyn shook her head. "I don't like the idea of this stuntman," she said for what seemed the hundredth time.

"Don't *worry* about him," Nikki insisted. "Who'd want a man like that? He falls on his head for a living."

THE LATE MORNING SUNLIGHT poured through the eastern windows.

Gil DeSpain stood before the mirror in the stuntman's trailer he shared with Carver, whose specialty was also horse work. Gil wore the scuffed black riding boots and dark blue trousers of a nineteenth-century cavalryman. He was shirtless, and he gritted his teeth as he retaped the jagged slash across his ribs.

The slash was from the hoof of a horse that had fallen when he'd tried to jump it across a gully and onto a steep incline. The horse had made the leap perfectly, but then lost its footing and gone down, scrambling madly.

Gil had sprung free to escape its crashing weight, but he couldn't roll away far enough to dodge its hooves. He'd struck an outcropping of rock with his shoulder, which was still black and blue. At almost the same moment the horse's hoof caught him in the side, opening a ten-inch gash.

He'd been mad, damned mad. He'd repeatedly told Fulton, the action director, that the horse needed dirt or sand on that slope to keep its footing. Fulton hadn't wanted to risk the chance of dust ruining the shot, but at last he'd agreed, and, like a fool, Gil had trusted him to keep his word.

But when the time came to film the scene, Fulton had reneged. When Gil and the horse hit the ledge, the stone was bare, and they'd fallen. The horse was badly hurt, perhaps ruined, and Gil had to be physically restrained—by three other stuntmen—from punching out Fulton.

His only satisfaction was that the director had fired Fulton, replacing him with a good stunt director, one Gil knew had sense. But it didn't make up for spoiling a good horse, which was a dirty, senseless shame. As for his own injuries, Gil shrugged them off. He was used to such things.

Carver lay on his bed, reading a girly magazine. Of all the stuntmen on location, he was second only to Gil in rank, but Gil didn't feel friendly toward him. Carver was fearless, but he was young, green and reckless. He was going to get hurt one of these days. Gil was not a betting man, but he would bet on that.

Carver lowered his magazine and watched Gil donning his dark blue officer's shirt. "So why don't you want to go to Reno over Thanksgiving?" Carver asked lazily. "I know these two show girls—sisters, twins, Trixie and Trudi. Beautiful girls. They'll give you something to be thankful for."

"Not interested," Gil said, fastening his cuffs. He was twenty-nine, almost ten years older than Carver. He was a tall man, lean but not lanky, every inch of him taut with hardened muscle.

The western sun kept him bronzed, even in November. He had dark brown, thick, wavy hair worn unfashionably long for the movie, and dark brown eyes that seemed permanently slitted against the sun. His cheekbones were high, his jaw hard, and his mouth gave the impression of being drawn permanently downward in a cynical slant.

His bone structure was enough like Gavin Chandler's that he could pass for him at a distance. It was in the particulars that their faces differed. Chandler's eyes were so blue, lucent and long-lashed they were almost girlish. Gil's were deep-set, guarded and dark. Chandler's lips were full and sensual. Gil's were narrower and more disciplined. There was no prettiness about him; rather, his features were marked by a certain angular harshness.

Gil had, in short, the sort of face that would make a careful man think twice before annoying its owner, but Carver was seldom careful.

"So why are you flying back to L.A. for the holidays?" Carver persisted. "You got something better than twin show girls? What? You been holding out on me?"

"Personal business," Gil said, tucking in his shirttail. Carver was nosy. It was one of his many failings.

"What sort of personal business?" Carver demanded, flipping through his magazine. "Don't tell me somebody's going to give you a shot at directing. I don't want to hear it. Lord, I'd hate to work for *you*." He shook his head and chuckled snidely. Gil was known for his perfectionism.

"Personal business," Gil repeated laconically.

He picked up his wide-brimmed officer's hat and put it on, tilting the brim low. He pulled on his gauntlets, picked up his gun and saber belts and slung them over his shoulder. No muscle in his face so much as flickered to show how close Carver had come to guessing the truth.

He opened the door of the trailer and stepped into the heat of the desert noon. The sunshine struck him like a slap, causing him to pull his hat brim even lower. He ambled across the sand toward the wardrobe trailer, the chains and spurs of his boots clinking.

He wasn't telling Carver the truth; he wasn't telling anybody. That was part of the deal. At first they'd offered money, and he'd said no. They offered more money. They got up to forty thousand. He had still said no.

"What do you want?" Gavin Chandler's representative had finally asked him in frustration and despair. The representative's name was Liveringhouse, and he had repeatedly phoned Gil from Hollywood. And, at last, Liveringhouse had given Gil the opening he'd waited for. "What do you want? Just tell me, what do you want?"

"I want to direct the action on Chandler's next picture," Gil had answered, his voice flat with matter-of-factness. "The sequel. I want charge of the second unit, the action unit."

"You can't," Liveringhouse had protested. "Chandler wants you to double for him—just you. You make him look good. You can't do all his stunts and direct, too."

"I don't have to do *any* of his stunts," Gil answered. "Stunt work I've got plenty of. I keep working—with Chandler or without him."

"Listen." Liveringhouse's voice was strained. "I *have* to get this one for Chandler. Caressa insists on it, and believe me, *nobody* wants to make this woman unhappy. I've got orders. You go to Vegas over Thanksgiving. Register as him. Draw the press away from him and Caressa. You're the only one who can do it. You look enough like him to be his brother. Nobody else could pull it off."

"Probably not," Gil said. The whole idea sounded stupid to him. He'd seen Caressa hanging around the sets on Chandler's last movie. This whole scheme was probably hers. She could play the press like a violin.

"Look—my job could be on the line." Liveringhouse was pleading now. "You stick around, cooperate, be a good guy, do what Chandler wants. You'll get your chance at second unit—eventually. Be reasonable."

"No," Gil said.

"Please? What if I beg you on bended knee? I know you can't see me, but—I swear this is true—I'm getting down on my knees right now. I'm *on* my knees. I'm *groveling*. I'm begging you on my knees. Go to Vegas for Chandler. How about for forty-five thousand? I'm on my knees, begging you to take this job for forty-five thousand dollars—begging."

Tears seemed to tremble in Liveringhouse's voice. "No," Gil said.

At last he got his way. He'd be in charge of the second unit on Chandler's next adventure epic, directing the action his way. And he didn't have to sell his soul to do it. All he had to do was spend five days in Vegas playing peekaboo with the press. Piece of cake.

He didn't know the woman pretending to be Caressa and didn't care. He intended to stay out of her way as much as possible. He hadn't cared much about women since Melly died. He doubted that he ever would again. He certainly wasn't interested in anybody who reminded him of Caressa.

Chandler's people had said she was a professional celebrity impersonator and that she could do an eerily accurate impression of Caressa. He'd asked if they were paying her a decent salary, and the answer was certainly. Gil assumed she'd get at least twenty thousand. He was well-acquainted with danger and precisely knew its monetary worth.

After all, the assignment was more than a little dangerous. Rumor ran that Caressa had been getting some particularly nasty threats since taking up with Chandler. The latest
curse of the celebrity was the jealous psychopath, and Caressa seemed to draw the type like a magnet. Her security
people were worried, and so were Chandler's.

Gil half suspected the farce in Las Vegas was less to di-
vert the press than to lure the loonies out into the open
where they could be caught. Chandler's people wouldn't
admit it, of course, and sounded nervous when Gil brought
up the idea. He'd mentioned it again this morning, after
learning the woman from New York would almost certainly be signed. Liveringhouse said she was only nineteen
or twenty. Gil didn't like that. He didn't like it at all.

"Has she been warned this could get dangerous?" he'd
asked.

"Of course." Liveringhouse's voice became silky. "We
wouldn't withhold anything. She's aware there are—haz-
ards."

"Good," Gil had said, setting his jaw. "Because I'm not
going to baby-sit her."

But now, as his easy stride took him to where the wardrobe trailer seemed to waver in the shimmering desert air, he
found himself wondering again about the woman. Matters
of security always obsessed him, especially since Melly, and
this job might well turn into a security problem.

Twenty years old was young—too young? How experienced was she? How professional? Could she think on her
feet? Could she take care of herself in a pinch?

As an impersonator, she came from the ragged fringes of
show business. He hoped she wasn't one of those star-struck
types who would spend the whole five days using her wiles
to cozy up to him, trying to cash in on his Hollywood con-
nections. Women like that abounded, and he loathed them
with all his flinty heart.

He pushed open the door of wardrobe and walked inside. The air-conditioned cool washed over him in a blessed wave.

Adelle, the wardrobe assistant, sat on a stool at the counter, taking a coffee break, poring over a tabloid. Her glasses were pushed far down on her snub nose, and she barely raised her head at his entrance.

"Hey, Adelle," he said out of the side of his mouth. "Put me to rights. Change me. Rearrange me. Have your way with me. I've got jumps to make and falls to take."

"Just a minute," murmured Adelle, her eyes skimming the paragraphs of the paper.

"What's so interesting?"

"Mmm." Adelle rose from the counter, but still couldn't drag her eyes from the tabloid. "Looks like he's really going to *do* it. Gavin Chandler. Marry her. Before the end of the month, this says."

Gil gave a dry, scoffing laugh. Adelle relished gossip.

"Don't laugh," Adelle said, looking up. "I know these rags make up half their news, but half is usually true. This says the gown's being designed and everything. They're really going to do it—tie the knot."

The lines at the edges of Gil's eyes crinkled at Adelle's seriousness. "Yeah? When? Where?"

"Probably Thanksgiving," she said, closing the paper. "And the smart money says Vegas. What a *shame.*"

Gil's smile faded. The publicity juggernaut and the security machinations had started in earnest. Even a person as well-versed in the ways of show business as Adelle was falling for the Vegas ploy.

"Why's it a shame?" he asked as she adjusted his sash and fastened his saber belt.

"It's a shame that Gavin's marrying *her,* that's what. He's a decent enough guy. Oh, I'd like to *shoot* her, that's what. So would every other red-blooded woman in America."

Gil was a man virtually without fear, yet her words sent a ghostly chill through him. After all, if the sweet, sane, sensible, motherly Adelle talked like this, what were the real loonies thinking?

"Don't say things like that," he muttered.

She ignored him and picked up his holster, inspecting it. "Oh, don't be so serious," she said. "You're always so serious."

But his frown stayed in place. It was his job to do dangerous things—and see that no one got hurt. The slash on his side pinched him with a twinge of pain, reminding him how easily things went wrong.

AT THAT MOMENT in New York, snow was falling thickly. Nikki stood, shivering, before the fried chicken restaurant near Radio City Music Hall, waiting for Roach to appear. She wore jeans and an old plaid jacket and tattered tennis shoes that let the snow seep in and numb her feet.

Her makeup, however, was perfect, just harsh enough to make her look a few years older. Despite the gray sky and snow, she wore sunglasses so that Roach wouldn't see the nervousness in her eyes.

True to his word, Roach appeared precisely at noon, rolling up in a gray limousine. The chauffeur leaped out and opened the door for her.

Nikki paused. Roach sat in the backseat like an elvish king in his coach. He wore a full-length coat of wolf skin and his expensively booted feet barely touched the floor. He looked even more wizened by daylight. He nodded for her to get in, and she did, settling into the seat across from him.

It didn't help Nikki's nerves that she had never before been inside a limousine. The car seemed more spacious than her apartment—it was intimidating. Roach made a spiraling movement with his finger, signaling the chauffeur to drive around the block a few times. Nikki swallowed hard.

She still wasn't sure she understood the contract, and she felt deeply unsettled, off balance. She wasn't even sure that if she was away from the familiar safety of the club's stage she could imitate Caressa.

But then she would remember Evelyn, tired, struggling not to slump in her wheelchair, and feel as if she had no choice. Evelyn was old, she was ill, she was tired and she was too busy taking care of everybody else to take care of herself. Nikki had to do something, and Roach was offering her the way to do it.

Wordlessly she handed him the contract she had signed.

Roach smiled for the first time. He had a tight, mirthless smile. "It's official." He plucked up the contract, thrust it into his briefcase and snapped it shut. The click sounded with dreadful finality in Nikki's ears.

He extended his hand and shook hers with false heartiness. "Congratulations," he said with his pinched smile. "You're going to Vegas for a white wedding."

Nikki said nothing. Her nerves quivered and twitched, and she tried to smile back.

"So—I'll be in touch with you," said Roach. "I'll pick you up a week from Tuesday—eight o'clock that night. You spend the night in Caressa's suite at the Plaza. I get *you* inside, then whisk *her* off."

Nikki nodded, but her eyes widened. "A suite? The Plaza? The *real* Plaza? On Fifth Avenue?"

"What Caressa does, she does in style. Wednesday morning, we get you to the airport, making sure you're just *glimpsed* by the press, of course—and that they know *exactly* where you're going—Vegas, of course. On Caressa's jet. You wear the white mink. It's more distracting."

Nikki nodded, but his words hardly registered. The familiar feeling of apprehension squeezed her stomach, and an aura of unreality settled over her.

Mink? A private jet? A suite at the Plaza?

It was happening, she thought numbly, it was really happening. She was going to impersonate Caressa in earnest. It had begun. She was so shaken that, for once, she couldn't even smile.

Across from her, Roach did smile in his stinting way, as if he knew something that she did not. But Nikki barely noticed. Her heart was beating too hard.

She would spend five days of her life pretending to be notorious.

Then she could spend the rest of her life being blessedly ordinary and unremarkable—like other people at last. And Evelyn could stop worrying about her.

"Here's a list of things to do before Monday," Roach said, handing her a folded sheet of paper. "Read it now if you want, in case there's anything you don't understand."

Nikki's blood froze. "I haven't got my glasses," she lied. "I'll read it later." She took the sheet of paper, folded it again and thrust it into her jacket pocket.

Her heart beat so fast it nearly choked her, but she tried to look more aloof than usual. She wondered if Roach suspected she had lied and decided from the self-absorbed look on his face that he did not.

Nikki had lied because she kept certain things secret from most people. The secret she guarded most closely was that she had a learning disability called dyslexia—word blindness. Although she had a high IQ, a quick mind and a remarkable memory, she could read only with the greatest difficulty. That was why Evelyn worried about her so much. If Roach had known, he probably never would have chanced hiring her.

But with twelve thousand dollars, Nikki could at last finish her special classes for dyslexics and train for a real job, a respectable job.

I'll be like other people. Like everybody else. It was the answer to all her prayers.

It was her heart's desire. And she was grabbing for it.

CHAPTER THREE

ON TUESDAY NIGHT, Nikki slipped, incognito, into the Plaza, and her own identity disappeared. On Wednesday morning, when she walked out, flanked by Roach and a brace of bodyguards, she had become Caressa. The transformation, with a silken dress designed for Caressa, Caressa's white mink coat and the star's own faux diamonds, was so complete it amazed and rather frightened Nikki.

Next, Nikki, who had never before been in a plane, found herself in Caressa's private jet. She was streaking toward Las Vegas, a city to which she had never been, to pretend to marry a man she had never met.

When the plane began its descent into Las Vegas, her stomach dipped with it. The apprehension she had successfully controlled for so long threatened to boil over, ungoverned. She squeezed her eyes shut, bit her perfectly made-up lip and prayed.

IN VEGAS, in the penthouse of the Xanadu Hotel, Gil DeSpain was having his own misgivings.

"What'd you do to your lips?" Liveringhouse demanded. "I wanted you to get collagen injections. I specifically requested you get collagen."

The two men sat in the gold and white splendor of the suite's sitting room. Liveringhouse, who wore an expensive three-piece suit and a Rolex watch, looked as if he belonged there.

Gil DeSpain did not. He sat on one of the white damask Grecian couches, bare-chested, untaping his latest cracked rib. He felt ludicrous. He wore skin-tight black leather pants, which he thought ridiculous, and cowboy boots made of python skin, which he thought criminal.

He clashed in spirit and appearance with the white carpets and fragile ormolu furniture with its white silk upholstery. He would have been happier alone, fishing in a swamp or in a mountain stream. He would have been happier alone anywhere, doing anything. Liveringhouse was getting on his nerves.

"I'm not having collagen shot into my lips," Gil sneered. "It's stupid. It's dangerous."

"Dangerous?" Liveringhouse's whine was indignant. "Yesterday you rolled down a mountain—six times. Six takes. You broke another damn rib. Last week a horse practically fell on you. You worry that *collagen's* dangerous?"

"I don't shoot chemicals into my body," Gil said. He stood and slipped into a blue silk shirt, the sort of expensive nonsense Gavin Chandler wore. Liveringhouse had become obsessed that Gil's bandages would show, since the shirt was meant to be worn buttoned only halfway up the chest.

"Your lips are too thin," Liveringhouse grumbled, eyeing Gil critically. "If you keep the sunglasses on, you can almost pass for him up close—except for the lips."

Gil threaded one of Chandler's opal-studded belts through the loops of the leather pants. "Chandler should have grown a mustache. With a mustache, I could pass."

"Caressa doesn't like mustaches," Liveringhouse said querulously. "You're going to have to keep your mouth covered if anybody gets close to you."

Gil fastened the belt's heavy silver buckle. It was a gaudy thing, studded, like the belt, with opals. The opals were

Australia's finest, but Gil didn't like them. Like many people whose business was risk, he believed in omens and portents. Opals were said to be unlucky. Lucky or not, this number of them was vulgar, and they seemed to symbolize the whole silly affair.

"We could put makeup on your lips," Liveringhouse suggested. He was a tall, fat man, soft and pale, and he wore horn-rimmed glasses. He leaned against the mantel, nervously tapping its gold-veined marble. "That'd do it—makeup."

"I'm not putting on makeup," Gil said contemptuously. "Forget it." He walked to a mirror and studied himself without amusement. Like most of Las Vegas, the palatial penthouse of the Xanadu was brilliant with mirrors.

He'd had his hair cut to a shorter length, a style imitating the one Chandler, who was currently playing an astronaut, now wore. He picked up a pair of Ray-Ban sunglasses such as Chandler favored and put them on. The illusion was rough, but real. From a distance he could pass for the Aussie.

Up close, his face was more weathered and the lips too cynical. The laugh lines bracketing his mouth were more deeply engraved, and his nose, once as straight and narrow as Chandler's, had been broken and had a slight bump at the bridge. But at a distance, he'd do.

Liveringhouse came to stand behind him, staring over his shoulder into the mirror. Liveringhouse had dark curly hair that dangled damply over his forehead in oiled tendrils. "We could say Chandler had an accident. We could bandage your lips." He put his hand on Gil's shoulder companionably, as if they were the finest of friends.

Gil's jaw went rigid in disgust. "Bandage my *lips?*"

"Sure," Liveringhouse said. "Listen. We could say Chandler cut himself shaving—"

Gil brushed the other man's hand away. "You are not," he growled, "going to bandage my lips." He swore, shaking his head. "This job is making you crazy, Liveringhouse, you know that?"

"Well, your lips are too *thin*," Liveringhouse fretted, turning to the fireplace. "Jeez, what if some photographer with a zoom lens uses it to zoom right in on your mouth? I mean, *I* have to think of things like that. *I* have to worry about details."

Gil turned and stared, unimpressed, out the room's enormous window. Far below the vivid green of hotel golf courses and lawns patched the autumnal brown of the desert, and buildings and cars and swimming pools winked bright colors in the sunlight. But beyond the city, the desert took over in earnest, a forbidding vista. It stretched out as stony, barren and dangerous as Gil's mood.

Liveringhouse glanced at his Rolex and then bit his thumbnail in nervousness. "She's late," he said, referring to Nikki who should have arrived with Roach half an hour ago.

"Then she's in character," Gil said out of the side of his mouth. "Caressa's always late."

"There's a guy up the twentieth floor of the Silverado," Liveringhouse muttered, chewing his thumbnail more savagely. He nodded toward the window where a neighboring hotel soared into the air. "He's a photographer. He's up there with a zoom lens, watching us. He's got his camera trained over her right *now*."

"I know," Gil said. "You've told me six times."

"He's going to zoom in on your *lips*," Liveringhouse said in a trembling voice. He pushed up his horn-rimmed glasses and seemed to wipe moisture from his eyes.

Gil stared at him in frustration, raked his hand through his unfamiliarly short hair. He threw the sunglasses on the couch in disgust.

He stepped up to Liveringhouse. This time it was he who put his hand on the other man's shoulder, but not with friendliness. He did it roughly enough to make Liveringhouse flinch, and he forced the younger, plumper man to face him.

"Look," Gil said, patience snapping, "you want me to have a fat lip? Just hit me, okay? No chemicals, no injections, no mad scientist doctor—just a nice clean punch in the mouth. Say Chandler was doing a fight scene and screwed up."

Liveringhouse recoiled in horror from the thought of violence. "Hit you?"

"Right," Gil said. "Right here. Go on. Then I won't have to listen to you snivel. Go on."

Liveringhouse backed away slightly, his soft mouth trembling. "I can't hit you. I might *hurt* you."

Gil looked at Liveringhouse's soft, pear-shaped body, at his pudgy white hand, so wrongly formed for punching. "It wouldn't hurt much. Just do it and shut up, will you?"

"You're crazy," Liveringhouse said, backing away another step. "You're really crazy, you know that?"

"No," Gil said flatly. "I'm tired. I'm tired of your whining and moaning. If you don't want to take a swing at me, then shut up about my lips—or I'll take a swing at *you,* Liveringhouse. I mean it."

"Oh, really," Liveringhouse said prissily. He made his escape to an armoire that hid the room's bar. He poured himself a glass of Scotch and drank it neat. He pressed his fingertips over his heart, as if measuring the healthiness of its beat. A look of even greater worry crossed his face. Liveringhouse was a notorious hypochondriac.

"This stress is killing me," he said. "My digestion is not good lately. Not good. When *she* gets here, I'm going to my room and have some stewed prunes sent up. My grandmother always says, 'Alvin, a prune is—'"

One of the gold phones rang, and Gil was spared Liveringhouse's grandmother's wisdom about prunes. Liveringhouse leaped toward the phone, snatching the receiver from the cradle. His round face quivered with nervousness. "Yes. Yes. Yes. Yes, *sir.*"

He hung up, adjusted his tie, checked his watch and cast Gil a harried look. "They're here. *She's* here. They're coming up on the service elevator. Listen. Go out on the veranda. She'll come out to meet you there. She's supposed to run into your arms. We know there's at least *one* photographer watching. If I know Roach, he's got a few more planted around. Make it romantic, all right?"

"I know the job," Gil said. He was sick to death of Liveringhouse's fretting.

"And keep your lips hidden, for heaven's sake," Liveringhouse begged. He picked up one of the hotel's gambling brochures from a desk. "Here. Hold this in front of your mouth. You know—like you're being thoughtful. Paul Newman uses that thoughtful pose a lot. So does Costner."

Gil shot Liveringhouse a threatening look, but it made no impact; Liveringhouse was too nervous. "Your Ray-Bans," Liveringhouse almost gibbered, "your *Ray-Bans!*"

With ill humor, Gil took the narrow brochure. He snatched the sunglasses, jammed them on and stalked to the roof garden, as much to escape Liveringhouse as anything else. He paced back and forth between plots of flowers, cacti and palms. The rooftop of the penthouse was as elaborate and lavish as its interior.

The private swimming pool glittered, turquoise-colored in the sunlight. An ingeniously contrived mock waterfall fed a cascade of blue water into the pool.

Statues of bronze and white marble ornamented the landscape. A small, artificial lagoon gleamed at the far edge of the roof, shaded by palm trees. Three white swans and a black one navigated its smooth surface. Peacocks strutted through the garden at the lagoon's edge. One screamed, a shrill, ominous sound.

Gil held the brochure near his mouth, tapping his chin with it. He tried to look as thoughtful as Prince Hamlet pacing the battlements of Elsinore. He glanced at the Silverado's twentieth floor, where he knew the photographer was watching. Grimly, he kept his mouth shielded.

He felt like a clown, a buffoon, in Chandler's clothing. He wondered why, so often, when fame checked into a person's life, taste immediately checked out. The pants were not only stupidly tight, they were uncomfortable. The shirt was opened halfway to his navel, and he had—indignity of indignities—a set of gold chains around his neck.

Gil paced, staring at the desert beyond the garish daytime glitter of Vegas. He stopped when he heard the door from the main sitting room open. Whispers sounded within the room. A slight twist of apprehension screwed within his stomach. He was no actor. He was used to the illusions of the movies, but his job was falling off horses and rolling down mountains and leaping off cliffs. He didn't do love scenes.

Then the woman appeared in the doorway, and although he thought he was prepared, he felt an unexpected jolt at the sight of her.

It was both Caressa and not Caressa. The mink, the cascade of crimped blond hair, the diamonds glinting in the sun, the way her lipsticked mouth curved, even her posture, all were startlingly familiar.

But beneath the makeup, her face was too fresh, too young, and in spite of the confident pose she struck, there was something hesitant, even shy, in her stiff body. It was Caressa as she might have been fifteen years ago, before she became as hard and guarded and expensive as the diamonds locked in her vault.

He looked at the woman, and she looked at him. He was conscious of the photographer spying on them from the Silverado, but even more conscious that the woman seemed to be freezing on him. He'd seen the phenomenon a dozen times on movie sets, and he recognized it. She was practically paralyzed by sudden fear.

He heard muted, anxious voices urging her to run to his arms. Liveringhouse's was loudest, a high-pitched, angry whine.

He forced himself to take a step toward her, although she should have been rushing toward him by this time. *Come on, kid,* he thought grimly. *Come to me. Make it look good. Do it.*

He took another step toward her.

"Caressa," he said, his harsh voice low. He held out his hand to her.

NIKKI HAD MADE IT exactly to the veranda door before the stage fright hit. Just as they'd entered the penthouse, Roach had handed her a scrawled note. Nikki had stared at it in panic.

If she were calm, if she had time, she might have made it out eventually. Under these conditions, and with Roach's ghastly handwriting, it was nearly impossible.

"I don't have my glasses," she hissed, pushing the note at him.

"Read it later," Roach ordered, refusing to take it.

Shaken, Nikki stuffed the note into the pocket of the mink. *I can't do this,* she thought, her self-confidence evaporating. Both Roach and the man called Liveringhouse began to bombard her with orders until her head buzzed with them.

Then, just as she stepped on to the veranda, the stage fright seized her. She'd never experienced it before, and it struck her as unexpectedly as a bolt of lightning from a clear sky.

The bright sun of Las Vegas blinded her, as did the glittering blue water of the pool and waterfall. Her knees felt no more substantial than the water trembling in that pool, and suddenly they would not carry her forward. *I can't do this,* she thought again in desperation. *How did I ever think I could do this? I'm on a roof with swans and a waterfall. Nothing makes sense.*

Her breath choked to a stop, filling her body with panic instead of air. Her nerve ends seemed to freeze and shrivel away painfully, torturing her with anxiety.

Still, somehow, as she stood in the doorway, she managed to strike a pose similar to one Caressa would strike. Roach had said that a photographer was set up, watching from a hotel across the way, and that he was the audience she must play to, the man she must make believe she was Caressa.

And that moment she believed she could fool nobody. And then she had seen a man by the pool, his back to her. Against the bright water and intense blue sky, he had been shadowy, a lean, dark shape without detail.

"Go to him," Roach had whispered behind her, his voice angry. "*Go* to him."

Her vision seemed to clear or adjust, but her heart beat just as wildly and sickly. Then the man turned and stared at her for what seemed an endless moment, and behind her the big man named Liveringhouse was hissing orders at her. But still she couldn't move.

The man on the veranda took a step toward her, and Nikki's heart leaped helplessly.

Oh, Lord, she thought helplessly. It *was* Gavin Chandler. The man had Chandler's wide shoulders, narrow hips, long legs. He dressed like Chandler; Chandler's brown hair, cropped short, gleamed in the beating sun, and Chandler's handsome face stared at her without expression.

Sunglasses hid his eyes, and for some reason he held a sort of brochure near his mouth, but she was convinced of it— it actually *was* Gavin Chandler, the movie star.

Somewhere, somehow, someone had made a terrible mistake. Her mind spun, all logic lost. She could never fool Chandler himself—what was Roach thinking of?

But the man took another step toward her, and he held out his hand as if in encouragement.

He both was Chandler, and yet he *wasn't*, Nikki suddenly thought in confusion; a dozen subtle differences crowded into her consciousness. But he was waiting for her, and she sensed he was trying to help her.

"Caressa," he said. The word brought her back to herself. The voice was not Chandler's. It was deeper, less measured, more rugged. It was unschooled in the art of theater and had no hint of an Australian accent.

Once more she was conscious of Roach and Liveringhouse behind her, rasping orders. She managed to take one hesitant step toward the man on the veranda. She tried to take a deep breath, but couldn't.

Then, suddenly, the man saved the situation. He was upon her, sweeping her into his arms, pulling her tightly against his half-bare chest.

"Loosen up, kid," he breathed as he bent over her. "It's only make-believe."

She had the fleeting impression of a sun-bronzed face descending toward hers.

Then she felt the heat of his kiss burning against her mouth like hard, sweet, life-giving fire.

CHAPTER FOUR

HIS MOUTH EXPLORED and claimed hers, warmly and with thorough expertise.

Disconcerted, Nikki squeezed her eyes shut, hoping darkness would clear her head. It did not. The stuntman's lean hands moved adeptly beneath her coat, caressing her body. She suddenly felt alarmingly bare beneath the silk, for Caressa never wore underwear.

Nikki was vaguely conscious that her sunglasses clacked against his and that one of his hands had moved up to her cheek, guiding her face more intimately toward his. He drew his mouth back only a fraction of an inch from hers. His breath was warm against her lips.

"Kiss me back," he ordered. "Put your arms around me."

Then his mouth captured hers again. Dazed, grateful for his coaching, but apprehensive, too, Nikki raised her arms and wound them around his neck.

"Are you DeSpain?" she whispered breathlessly, when his mouth traveled to the curve of her throat.

"Right." He kissed her behind the ear, drawing her so close she could feel the strong beat of his heart against her breasts.

"Pleased to meet you," she managed to say, tightening her arms around his neck.

"Same to you," he said. Then he kissed her until she had the strange sensation that the earth was falling away and the sky was turning inside out.

With extraordinary make-believe passion, he pushed the mink coat from her shoulders so that they were bared to the cool autumn air. His hands ran possessively over their smoothness, warming her and chilling her at the same time.

Once more his mouth traveled down her throat until it pressed the edge of the dress's low neckline, in the shadowed valley between the swell of her breasts. "Drop the coat," he murmured, his breath tickling her skin.

Good theatrical gesture, she thought dazedly, and lowering her arms, she let the coat slide to the stones of the veranda. Dropping the coat seemed a shameful way to treat so expensive an object, but was exactly the sort of careless, dramatic act in which Caressa specialized.

"Now," he said softly, his mouth moving up her throat, "put your arms around me again."

She did so. His lips gently grazed the edge of her jaw, and all thoughts of the mink fled her mind. She gasped as his mouth found hers again, and he swept her up into his arms as easily as if she were weightless. He whirled her around slowly, once, then twice, still kissing her.

His lips never left hers, even when he strode toward the penthouse and kicked open the door that led to one of the bedrooms. He carried her inside, pausing only long enough to kick the door shut again behind them before heading toward the canopied bed.

Then, unceremoniously, he released her, dumping her on the king-size bed. She bounced, sitting up, and blinked at him in confusion. He took off his sunglasses, clamped his mouth into a stern line and thrust out his hand.

Nikki stared at him, her heart racketing against her rib cage. She felt giddy, as if her life was a film running backward. This man had just kissed her senseless and carried her to bed. Now he offered her the most businesslike of handshakes.

Hesitantly, she took his hand, which was brown, lean, hard with muscle and marked by innumerable small scars.

"Sorry about all the mouth contact," he said brusquely. "They don't like my lips."

Nikki wondered how anyone could not like his lips. He had a strong mouth, narrow but well-shaped, full of character and hinting at cynical humor. Her mouth still tingled from its touch, and she could not help wondering what his kisses would be like if he meant them. The thought caused an unsettling flutter in the pit of her stomach.

She turned her attention from his lips to his eyes, which unlike Gavin Chandler's world-famed blue ones were dark, and not dreamy but startlingly alert.

"Didn't mean to come on too strong, either," he said, releasing her hand. "I got the feeling you froze."

Nikki smiled a nervous, aloof smile. She looked away from the steadiness of his gaze, ashamed of her moment of fear. "It won't happen again. I promise you that. You can depend on me."

She meant it. The sudden attack of stage fright had both humiliated and terrified her. She was grateful to Gil De-Spain for spotting her problem. But she wished Roach had told her how attractive DeSpain was. He was much nicer-looking, Nikki thought, than the too-perfect handsomeness of Gavin Chandler. "Thank you," she added. She made her voice reserved, but her heart kept pummeling.

DeSpain turned from her and shrugged. "Forget it."

He checked the drapes veiling the door to the veranda, making sure they were completely shut. Satisfied, he turned to her again, studying her with his unreadable dark eyes.

"You want this bedroom?" he asked. "It's the biggest of four. I don't care which one I have."

She watched him almost furtively, still shamed by her stage fright, still surprised at the sort of man he seemed to be. Although clearly an outdoor sort, he had a practical, strictly business air. He wore the form-fitting black pants and half-open shirt easily, but with careless disdain, as if they were a costume he found slightly ridiculous.

Roach scuttled into the bedroom, carrying the mink coat. The tall, unpleasantly plump man named Liveringhouse followed. Roach looked irritable, and Liveringhouse's face was mottled with anger. He glared at Nikki.

"What's the matter with you?" Liveringhouse demanded, pointing at her. "Is that the best you can do? You went out that door and stood there like a bump on a log. If I tell you to move, girly, you *move*. If you can't be professional about this, we replace you. It's not impossible."

"I'm sorry," Nikki said stiffly, for Liveringhouse's tone angered her. "I was—disoriented."

"Make damned sure you don't get disoriented again," Liveringhouse warned, his face hostile.

Nikki started to say something in her own defense, but Gil DeSpain spoke instead. His voice was quiet, easy, yet somehow danger resonated in it.

"Lay off, Liveringhouse. We had to do it cold, no rehearsal. Besides, I should have gone to her. It makes more sense."

Liveringhouse looked sullen, almost pouty, but said no more. Nikki wondered if he was a bit afraid of DeSpain. Liveringhouse took his displeasure out by glaring at her, and Nikki, offended, stuck her nose slightly in the air, not trusting herself to speak. She wished her pulses would slow to a sensible rate.

Roach held the coat toward her and shook it. His withered face was pale. "And don't drop Caressa's coat. Do you know how much this thing cost?"

"I told her to drop it," Gil said with the same chilling quiet. "It's the kind of thing Caressa would do."

Liveringhouse nodded. "Affirmative. Dropping the coat was a good move. Makes a more dramatic picture. My man is right. Chandler can have the coat cleaned."

Roach scowled at Liveringhouse. "Caressa can afford to have her own coat cleaned," he said with more than a touch of acid. He threw the coat on the bed beside Nikki. "Hang this up. And take it *easy* with it from now on."

Nikki nodded coolly but didn't touch the coat. She didn't intend to until Roach was out of the room; she would not jump to carry out his commands. "What's next on the agenda?" she asked, her voice clipped and no-nonsense.

"For one thing, you don't freeze up again," Liveringhouse said nastily.

"I *said* it won't happen again," she retorted, resolving it wouldn't. She wouldn't give either Roach or Liveringhouse the satisfaction.

Roach shook his head, disgust on his narrow face. "Lie low. At four o'clock, you go out—incognito, but not incognito, if you know what I mean. Buy a marriage license. You'll use their real names. Then get straight back here. We've got a plant over at the license place. He leaks the word immediately, the press finds out. Tonight, keep to yourselves. Go out on the veranda from about ten until eleven—give the photographer over there an eyeful. Play kissy face. Like you can't keep your hands off each other."

In spite of her resolve to be undaunted, Nikki bit the corner of her lower lip. She slid another furtive glance toward Gil and was disconcerted to find his dark eyes fastened on her face. The ghost of a derisive smile played with the normally severe line of his mouth.

Quickly she looked away. "Kissy face," she said with distaste. She looked at her gloved hands in her lap. The false diamonds on her wrists flashed, mocking her with their unreality.

"Your luggage is on the way up," Roach said, ignoring her protest. "The bellman is an informer for the *National Inquisitor*. We can use him, but we have to be careful. You," he said, pointing at Nikki, "keep your mouth shut. I'll do the talking. Let him see you. That's all."

Roach turned to Gil, eyeing him as if he didn't trust him. "Weren't you supposed to do something about your lips? What is this?"

Liveringhouse looked righteous and disapproving. "I *told* him to do something. I expressly asked it. He won't."

"Why not?" Roach demanded, glowering at Gil.

Gil's expression turned to bored irritation. "I'm sick of the subject." He shrugged and began unbuttoning his shirt. He walked out of the bedroom and into an adjoining one.

"Where are you going?" Roach barked after him. "I want you in the room with her when that bellhop shows up. Just keep your face away from him—understand?"

Gil, already out of sight, didn't bother to answer. Nikki smiled at his boldness.

Roach wheeled to face Liveringhouse. "He's a trouble-maker, that one. I don't like his attitude. If you can't keep him under control—"

"I *can* keep him under control," Liveringhouse countered, his oily black curls shaking in indignation. "What I *don't* need is you throwing your weight around, trying to undermine my authority. DeSpain at least is a professional. This—this *kid,*" he said with a contemptuous gesture toward Nikki, "freezes as soon as the chips are down. You'd better worry about her and let me handle DeSpain."

"Yeah?" countered Roach, staring up at the younger man. "Well, if you can handle him, go do it. I want him here when that bellhop comes. If you can't do your job right, I'll tell Caressa—and she'll see you don't *have* a job."

Liveringhouse, looking angry but also frightened, stalked off after Gil. Roach turned his reptilian gaze to Nikki.

"Take the gloves off. You're supposed to be sharing this place with your lover. Look like it, will you?"

Nikki tossed her chin, stood and stripped off one long glove, then the other. She unfastened a bracelet. "You and Liveringhouse are both rude," she said evenly. "You seem to forget that you have to depend on us—on DeSpain and me. You ought to remember that. Things might go better for all of us."

Roach's small eyes nearly rolled in aversion. "Now you're *talking* like her. I hate this whole ridiculous charade," he muttered. "I hate it." He left the room. Nikki heard him in the main sitting room, mixing a drink.

She looked about the bedroom, feeling more disoriented than before. The suite at the Plaza had been lavish. The penthouse seemed more opulent still, and from the little Nikki had seen, its decor changed from room to room.

The main sitting room was all white and gold, lushly simple. The bedroom, however, overwhelmed her with its richness. It was Oriental in splendor, with a motif of peacocks. Silks of pale iridescent blue covered the walls, those of darker blue and green draped the giant canopy bed.

The thick blue-green carpet was strewn with Oriental rugs, and on one wall glittered a mosaic of gold tiles and semiprecious stones. It depicted a maharaja's courtyard, with jeweled peacocks and fountains spouting silver. Nikki had never seen such a room, not even in a picture.

She touched the filagreed curves of a chair, wondering if it was plated with real gold.

The room could have been garish, but was not. Each detail was so sumptuous and well-crafted that the impression was of wealth and luxury. Jeweled mirrors gleamed softly from almost every nook.

From what Nikki could see of the bathroom, there was another peacock mosaic and additional mirrors. And, from every mirror into which she glanced, she saw not herself, but Caressa, looking uncharacteristically unsure of herself.

Pull yourself together and stay that way, Nikki told herself sternly. Taking a deep breath, she squared her chin, and half a dozen mirrors told her that she was doing better. She took off her faux diamond earrings and lay them on the nightstand next to the bracelets.

Going to the nearest mirror, she examined her eye makeup. It seemed fine. Worried, she adjusted her hair. Roach had had it cut and styled this morning at the Plaza, in the suite. He'd even summoned a manicurist. This morning he'd given her the dress, which was of peacock blue silk, and the white mink coat, as well as all the jewels.

Now he wanted her to look like a glamorous woman, happily settling in with her lover. How would such a woman look? Nikki didn't know. None of Rhonda's love affairs had been glamorous, and none had been happy.

She pulled a stray blond curl over her eyes and forced her lips into a pouty smile, testing it. She took off two of the rhinestone necklaces, but left on the third, the simplest, its single pendant hanging between her breasts.

She kicked off her shoes, which left her barefoot, for Caressa never wore stockings. She pushed down the left strap of the blue silk dress. Her lipstick was smudged from Gil DeSpain's kisses, and her mouth still pulsed and tingled from his touch. She was surprised to realize she found the tingle pleasurable. She had seldom allowed herself to be kissed before. She had never found it agreeable.

But the lipstick needed repair, so she padded barefoot into the bathroom. An array of expensive cosmetics and perfumes lined the marble dressing counter, waiting for her. Beside them was English shaving soap, after-shave and a man's cologne. For Chandler. No—for Gil. The intimacy of the arrangement sent an odd frisson through her.

Years had passed since Nikki had lived near a man. She didn't remember her own father and all she recalled of Aunt Rhonda's husband was that he was a shadowy, undependable figure. Nikki wanted to forget as much as possible about Rhonda's boyfriends; they were a bad lot, and remembering them chilled her.

She pushed the memory of them from her mind; she was skilled at it. Uncapping the lipstick, she took up a lip brush and began to recreate Caressa's perfect mouth.

A distant knock sounded at the main entrance of the sitting room, and she stiffened, knowing it must be the bellman. The bathroom door was ajar. If the bellman brought her luggage into the bedroom, he'd catch a glimpse of her standing before the jeweled bathroom mirror. Would that be enough?

She heard both Roach and Liveringhouse trying to give the bellman orders at once. Then the other bedroom door swung open, and Gil, shirtless, his lower face covered with shaving cream, entered her bedroom.

He gave Nikki a slanting, ironic smile as he came into the bathroom and stood beside her. Although the room was large, spacious in the extreme, it seemed to contract when he was so close. She could smell the tangy scent of the soap on his jaw, sense the pulsing heat of his naked skin.

"Look—no lips." He gestured at his lathered face. "I can pass for Chandler—or a rabid dog." He made a humorous growl so deep that Nikki shivered.

She made a move to close the bathroom door a bit more, and he nodded. "But not all the way. Relax. Let him see us. I'll keep my profile to him, so he can't see me full face. Why don't you stand behind me, put your arms around my waist? That way some of my scars will be hidden. Make it look cozy. Give him a look at us he'll remember."

Nikki stared into the reflection of Gil's eyes in the mirror. They were such dark eyes, their gaze so steady that, although she trusted few people, she wanted to trust him. She appreciated his ability to improvise a scene, but felt shy about doing as he suggested.

He seemed to sense her nervousness. "Come on. I'm not really a mad dog. I don't bite. Here. For the sake of realism."

He bent and kissed her left shoulder, the nearly bare one. His lips were warm, his lathered jaw moist and cool. He left a snowy white badge of shaving soap on her skin.

"Not bad," he said, examining it critically. "But I can see greater vistas for realism. Come here. Chandler's the type to brand his woman."

He took her face in his lean hand, bent and kissed her cheek with maddening lightness, then drew away half-smiling. Nikki's heart lurched.

She heard the bellman pushing his loaded luggage cart toward the room, saw the bedroom door opening. Glancing in the mirror again, she saw a dab of Gil's lather on her cheek.

"Now hug me from behind," he whispered. "Not too hard. I've got a cracked rib."

Quickly Nikki moved behind him and slipped her arms around his waist. He had an extraordinarily lean waist, his stomach plated with muscle. A fresh scar shone palely across his ribs, its surface smooth beneath her fingertips.

She heard the soft clatter of the bellman's cart as he entered the bedroom. Roach's wheedling voice drew nearer as well, peppering the bellman with orders.

"Now," Gil said softly, "all you have to do is pretend to enjoy it. Ham it up, kid."

He drew the razor slowly along the edge of his jaw. Nikki sensed the bellman's prying eyes on them and pressed her cheek against Gil's tanned shoulder blade. "I'm afraid I'll make you cut yourself," she whispered, her lips almost touching the sinewy hardness of his back.

She felt his body shake as he gave a silent laugh. He turned so his face was away from the bellman and whispered over his shoulder: "Are you crazy? You think I've got a *blade* in this thing?"

Nikki smiled, relaxing a bit. A muscle in his back twitched when her breath touched it. She hugged him more tightly and pressed her cheek more affectionately against his shoulder blade. Somehow it did not seem an unlikely gesture. His muscle twitched again, as if teasing her or excited by her touch.

It's only make-believe, she told herself.

She closed her eyes and snuggled nearer because she knew the bellman was watching, greedy for details. She wondered if she could be allergic to the scent of Gil's shaving lather, for it seemed to make her dizzy. She resisted the impulse to hug him more tightly to keep her balance.

"Mmm," he said, as if coaching her.

"Mmm," she echoed. Slowly, almost lazily, she opened her eyes, trying to make herself look as languid as Caressa.

Her gaze met the frankly curious one of the bellman. He was a small, thin man of indeterminate age, with a pointed nose and chin that gave him a ratlike air.

He stared at Nikki and Gil with something akin to predatory triumph. If he was, as Roach claimed, an informer for the *Inquisitor,* he must be thinking he had gone to informer heaven—Caressa and Gavin Chandler snuggling before his eyes, in the private bath of their jeweled bedroom.

In his hands, the bellman held a long clothing bag, which he had let sag slightly toward the floor. Roach shook the man's shoulder. "Don't let it crumple, you idiot—that's her gown. Here—let me see—fool."

Nikki's eyes widened as Roach jerked the bag away and unzipped it. From it he drew a long white dress, obviously a wedding gown. Roach pretended to inspect it, then hung it in the closet.

The bellman's expression grew more crafty. He was obviously adding up the elements, and the sum was clear. A marriage license could be had more swiftly and easily in Nevada than any other state. Vegas plus Caressa plus Chandler plus wedding gown could equal only one thing: the fabled marriage was really about to take place. The bellman knew he could get a fat price for such information.

Roach dug into his pocket, withdrawing a fifty dollar bill. "Don't get any ideas about this," he warned the bellman, giving a careless wave in the direction of the dress. "It's a prop, that's all. We're making a video here. So keep your mouth shut. We don't want people getting the wrong idea."

Nikki knew that Roach's express purpose was exactly that—to give people the wrong idea. She watched as the bellman pocketed the bill, then turned to stare at her and Gil again, greed in his little rodent eyes.

Worried that she would betray herself, she turned her face away from the bellman and Roach, laying her other cheek against Gil's back. Her arms tightened around his waist, and she felt a sudden, slight intake of his breath. She winced, hoping she hadn't hurt his injured rib.

"Sorry," she whispered against the bare skin of his shoulder blade.

"It's okay," he muttered under his breath, but his voice was tight.

Relief flooded through Nikki as she realized Roach was at last ushering the bellman out of the room. She felt a sense of deliverance as she heard the door closing behind the two men. Immediately she released Gil and stepped backward swiftly, as if to apologize for having touched him.

Her knees felt powerless, and her heart pounded as she sagged against the glittering mosaic of peacocks. Gil turned, taking a towel and wiping the last vestiges of soap from his face. "Thank God he left." He smiled his half-serious smile. "I was running out of lather. Fooled him, didn't we?"

She nodded, still trying to catch her breath. "I'm sure of it. But this is harder than I thought."

"You were fine," he said, setting down the razor. He patted her on the arm, a gruff, almost brotherly gesture. He tossed her the towel. "Here. Wipe your shoulder."

She dabbed at the lather on her shoulder, glad to look at something besides the brown expanse of Gil's chest. The lather on her cheek was gone; she'd streaked it across his shoulder blade. She thought of offering to wipe it away for him, but was too shy.

The bathroom door swung open more widely, and Liveringhouse loomed there, looking angrily at Nikki. "You call that lovey-dovey?" he demanded. "Just standing there with your arms around him? I watched from the other room—you call that being a sex goddess?"

Nikki gritted her teeth and shot him a resentful look.

"She was fine," Gil repeated, taking the towel from Nikki and tossing it over his shoulder. "Back off, Liveringhouse."

Roach scurried up behind Liveringhouse, looking at Nikki over the larger man's shoulder. "It was all right, but just all right—no more," he said, his thin face stern. "You—" he pointed to Nikki "—put more into it. More *oomph*. Didn't you read my note? You should have been kissing his back, touching him more. Like you were trying to drive him crazy. Not just hugging him like some—some kid with her teddy bear."

Nikki seldom blushed, but she blushed at Roach's words. She'd forgotten about the note, and she suddenly felt stupid and defenseless. She couldn't let Roach know about her dyslexia. She didn't want any of these strangers to know.

Besides that, she had just met Gil DeSpain. Hugging him was difficult enough. Kissing him all over to drive him crazy was out of the question.

After a few ugly encounters with Rhonda's boyfriends, Nikki had perfected the art of resisting advances. She had purposely never cultivated the art of inviting them. She thought she had been almost wanton with Gil. Now the other men acted as if she was laughable, amateurish.

Gil put his hands on his hips and stared at Liveringhouse and Roach. "I'll tell you what," he drawled. "We're supposed to be honeymooners, right? It *might* work better if you two got out of here and let us at least get to know each other. Besides, I've got a cracked rib, remember? I *told* her to take it easy, dammit."

Roach's nostrils flared, but he took a step backward. "Fine," he snorted. "Get to know each other. But don't either of you go anywhere or be seen without me saying so."

"Without *us* saying so," Liveringhouse interjected. He drew himself up so that he towered even higher than usual over the smaller, sparer man.

"I know my job," Gil said. Without further ceremony, he shouldered past the two men into his bedroom, disappearing. Nikki was sorry to see him go. He seemed her only ally.

When Roach and Liveringhouse finally left for their rooms on the floor beneath, however, she wasn't at all sorry. She didn't know which of the two men she liked least.

She went to the bed and picked up the mink coat from the peacock-colored spread. She drew out the note, unfolded it and shook her head. Roach's writing was such a set of chicken scratches, she would never have puzzled it out in the time she had, and now it was too late. She crumpled it, and flung it into a jeweled wastebasket.

Nikki hung the coat in the closet on a padded hanger beside the white bridal dress, then paused, wondering if she dared touch so elegant a gown.

Carefully, almost guiltily, she drew out its skirt to examine it more closely. It wasn't the sort of dress she would have expected. It struck her as far too traditional for Caressa, who never followed fashions, but always set them.

The gown had long sleeves, elegantly puffed at the top and a simply cut neck. The lower sleeves and bodice were encrusted with seed pearls and inset with lace. The pearls and lace reappeared on the long, full skirt, cascading beautifully down its folds. It was a lovely dress, but at the same time almost demure.

Nikki sighed in puzzlement as she let the skirt drop gently into place. She couldn't imagine Caressa, the queen of sex, transformed into a virginal maiden.

Nikki's problem, of course, was the reverse, to transform herself into a sex goddess, and she wondered for the hundredth time if she could possibly succeed. It was easy to look like Caressa. To act like Caressa was another matter.

Nikki shook her head wearily and ran her hands through her crimped blond hair. Suddenly she realized that she had a headache and that she was hungry. She'd been too nervous to eat anything since last night.

A clean face might help clear her mind, she thought, moving to the bathroom to wash away the thick makeup. And rest—she hadn't slept well for the last week.

She turned a golden faucet and ran the water until it gurgled out icy cold. It felt blessedly cool and clean, and she closed her eyes, relishing its purifying power.

It wouldn't even be so difficult to pass for Caressa if she could do it alone, she thought, her head still pounding. But to have to do it with Gil DeSpain seemed degrading. He seemed like a gentleman, and she didn't like acting like a floozy every time she was near him. It embarrassed her, made her feel cheap.

Nikki buried her face in the softness of a blue-green towel, remembering how it felt to touch his half-bare body, her cheek pressed against the strong hardness of his back. Her blood coursed in confusion. She hadn't imagined liking being so near a man—not after the incidents in her past. She didn't *want* to like it.

A knock on the frame of the partly open bathroom door made her look up, blinking wildly. She was so weary of the unexpected that every new thing startled her clear to her marrow. Suddenly all she wanted was to be home in the Village, safe and alone.

But she wasn't alone. Gil DeSpain lounged in the doorway, studying her with his intent dark eyes. Her heart took an unexpected flying leap into space.

He had changed clothes and now wore blue jeans, low-slung and faded. A battered belt had replaced the one studded with opals. His chest was safely covered by a dark blue plaid shirt that looked as well-worn as the jeans. He had exchanged the flashy boots for ones of brown scuffed leather.

Gil stood with his arms crossed, leaning against the door frame. "So that's what you really look like," he said in his low, slow voice.

He had a strange twist to his mouth that at once seemed to be both a smile and not a smile. "My God," he said. "You're only a kid. You're not even twenty—how old are you?"

"I'm twenty-one," she protested, too shaken by his sudden appearance to lie. She sometimes added several years to her age, sometimes subtracted them—whatever it took to make her feel safer.

His mouth twisted more enigmatically. "A kid," he repeated, shaking his head.

But when he looked her up and down in his deliberate way, she didn't feel like a child. She felt like a woman. It was a disconcerting feeling, new, a sensation she had been told never to trust.

Hurriedly she reached for a tube of lipstick. She didn't like him seeing her naked face; she never let anyone see it.

Always she wore a mask of some sort to confront the world. She kept her real self hidden, and she was embarrassed to be caught without a disguise of any kind.

He reached out, his hand clamping over hers, gently but with irresistible firmness. "No," he said, studying her face intently. "Don't cover yourself up with artificial things. Why would you ever change such a face?"

She tried to draw her hand away, but he held it fast. His touch made strange sensations course through her like electricity, prickling her blood. She laughed uneasily.

"It's my job. I'm supposed to look like other people."

"Not now," he said, his hand tightening around hers. "Not with just me. Let me see the real you."

"No," said Nikki, extricating her hand from his. She made her voice standoffish. "There is no real me. Don't bother looking for one."

Her heart beat too fast for comfort. She leaned toward the large mirror and sketched a new mouth for herself, a thinner, more controlled, harder one than her own.

CHAPTER FIVE

GIL DIDN'T LIKE living in this hall of mirrors. The countless images reflected each other endlessly, tricking the eye and toying with the mind. He was an outdoor man, a man of action, who felt locked in a claustrophobic fun house.

Neither did he like what Nikki was doing to her face, so he frowned. The frown was for himself, as well; he hadn't meant to touch the woman and wished he hadn't. The contact had sent an unexpected fire racing through him.

He had been determined to ignore her for the most part. But she wasn't what he had expected, not at all.

She was scared by the whole situation, he could tell. He could also tell she wasn't about to quit. She was driving herself by sheer force of nerve, and there was a militance, a toughness in her stance before the mirror. He didn't know if she'd taken on the tough air to fool him or to fool herself.

The glimpse he'd had of her bare face intrigued him. She had a clean-cut, delicate prettiness that had caught him off guard. Her skin was clear, slightly tawny, and her nose was flecked with the faintest of freckles.

Her mouth was wide, generous and formed for smiling. But he'd never seen her smile. She had beautiful, winglike eyebrows, darker than her blond hair, and her lashes were darker still. Her eyes, smoky autumn blue, puzzled him most. They were beautiful eyes, both wary and eager, knowing and innocent. They were eyes full of paradoxes and, he suspected, secrets.

She picked up an eyeliner pencil and began to make them into a different sort of eyes, older and harder. He wanted to take her hand again, to stop her, but he didn't.

Nikki glanced at his reflection in the mirror, meeting his gaze. "Stop staring," she ordered. Her tone was aloof, but nervousness played around her mouth. "What are you doing here, anyway? Did you ever hear of knocking?"

He crossed his arms again and raised an unrepentant eyebrow. "I knocked. I also called. The water was running. You didn't hear. You didn't lock the bedroom door—and you didn't close this one."

She darted him a distrustful glance, then finished putting on her eyeliner. He watched as she applied mascara, covering the natural silkiness of her lashes with a thick coat of black. It irked him that she seemed suspicious of him. Did she place him in the same class as Roach and Liveringhouse?

"So," he said with a careless shrug, "do you want to get acquainted? Other than physically? It might help."

"Help what?" Nikki asked warily.

"This all seems to make you nervous," he answered, looking her up and down. The blue silk dress, with its thin straps and plunging neckline, had looked like a costume on her when she was bare-faced. But now she was creating a face that went with it.

She raised one shoulder in a shrug. "Who wouldn't be nervous?" she asked, still sounding on guard against him. "This isn't exactly how everybody spends the holidays."

"You look like her," he mused, then corrected himself. "No—you can *make* yourself look like her. You do it on stage, they said. You shouldn't be nervous on that count."

"This isn't a stage."

"Shakespeare said that all the world's a stage."

"I don't know what Shakespeare said," Nikki answered, her voice even. "I'm not the theatrical type."

"You're a performer."

She shrugged again, almost with contempt. It made him notice how smooth and golden her shoulders were, how her breasts moved freely and without confinement.

"No. I'm not. Looking like her—it's just something that I learned. A trick. Like wiggling your ears."

He shook his head dubiously. "They said you worked in a club."

"I do. Would you *please* stop staring at me? It's getting on my nerves."

"Sorry." He turned and regarded the Oriental richness of the bedroom. He didn't like the new face she was creating, anyway. He'd been searching for traces of the old one.

"So why are you doing this?" he asked, looking at the jeweled peacock on the bed's silken canopy. "You're not looking for your break into the big time?"

"No." She said it with such force, such certainty, that he couldn't help glancing at her again.

She stood, a powder puff in her hand, her makeup completed, perfect. Somehow, he thought, she'd managed to obliterate almost every trace of her own personality. Her new face was older and more sophisticated than her own, a perfectly acceptable face, he supposed, but not really *hers*.

"This isn't your ticket to stardom?" he persisted. "What is it then?"

"Just the opposite," Nikki said, pulling her hair into a simple ponytail and fastening it. "The last thing I want is to be a *star*. I want *out* of this crazy business. Excuse me."

As she made her way past him, her naked shoulder skimmed the sleeve of his shirt. The scent of Caressa's expensive perfume floated behind her and tingled in his nostrils. She went to the closet, drew out an oversize blue shirt and slipped it on over the silk dress.

"Is there any food around here?" she asked, as she buttoned the shirt to the throat. "I'm starved."

Gil gave her a measuring look. Although her face now seemed artificial and her hair made her look almost severe, her body reminded him of a teenage girl dressed incongruously in her mother's dress and her father's shirt. She sent out more contradictory signals than any woman he'd ever met.

"There's a kitchen, but no cook," he said. "All these bedrooms have bars. The sitting rooms have bars and minifridges." He changed the subject. "You've got a strange sense of fashion, if you don't mind my saying so."

"These aren't my clothes," Nikki said defensively, looking down at the big shirt. "I'm a prisoner of *her* wardrobe. I'd kill for some underpants. Those refrigerators—is there anything like a sandwich in one of them?"

"Something vaguely like a sandwich." He strolled to the door to the sitting room and opened it, nodding an invitation to her to enter. "Caressa and Chandler are both healthfood nuts. Come on. You can have some nice bean sprouts and tofu."

Nikki's shoulders sank unhappily. "You mean there's no real food? We have to eat health food for five days? I'll starve."

Gil's mouth crooked slightly. "It's part of the illusion. If Caressa and Chandler were here, they'd demand to have the right food waiting for them. Come on. What's wrong with a little turnip juice?"

Dismay crossed her perfectly made up face. "The whole nation's about to sit down to turkey and dressing, and I'm stuck here with granola." Her posture grew mournful. The big shirt's cuffs dangled over her fingertips, making her seem more of a puzzling amalgam of woman and child than before.

Stop watching her as if she's some sort of fascinating creature, Gil warned himself.

"Sit down," he muttered, his tone gruff. "You want a peanut butter and jelly sandwich? Some carrot sticks? A ginseng soda?"

"Peanut butter and jelly?" She brightened.

Her reaction made him change his assessment of her yet again. He told himself she *was* only a kid, an inexperienced kid, and his job was to steer her through the idiotic maze before them.

"Sit," he repeated. "I'll make it. I'm not used to being cooped up. It makes me restless."

She sat carefully on the edge of the white Grecian couch. He made her a sandwich, put some carrot sticks beside it and opened the soda.

"Thanks," she said, when he set everything on the coffee table before her. "You may have saved my life."

He sat across from her in a chair so delicate and pristine it added to his edginess.

The sandwich looked unappetizing, but she attacked it with fervor.

"You don't look like a peanut butter and jelly kind of girl," he offered, "with all that makeup. Why wear it?"

"I can't believe this is what they eat," Nikki said, ignoring his question. "Just health food? This is really how the beautiful people live?"

He nodded. "Yes. Because they want to stay beautiful forever. Now tell me, why are you doing this? If you're not interested in show business."

Nikki jolted him with her disconcertingly blue gaze. Once more he had the impression that her eyes seemed both young and old.

"I *don't* want to be in show business," she said emphatically. "I'm doing this for the money, that's all. So I can get *out*. Away from craziness like this."

After she finished the last carrot stick, she set down her empty plate and wiped her hands clean. They were lovely hands, and remembering them moving shyly against his bare flesh made him take his breath in so sharply that it hurt his cracked rib.

"Get out? To what? Where?"

She put her hand to the tightly buttoned collar of her shirt. "New Jersey," she said, her voice defensive again. "Gooseburg, New Jersey."

He couldn't help it. He laughed. She looked affronted.

"What's so funny?" she asked.

"Pretty girls head for Broadway or Hollywood—or even here, Vegas. Not Gooseburg, New Jersey. What's in Gooseburg?"

"A makeup salon," she said in the same wary tone. "And boutique. Women get their faces done. And buy cosmetics."

"You're going to *buy* this place?"

"No," she said coolly. "Just work there. I've always aspired to live in a place named Gooseburg."

She dusted a few crumbs from her lap, rose and went to the window. She stood staring out at the desert beyond the sun-struck limits of the city.

He narrowed his eyes, taking stock of her. For a few moments, while she ate, she had been almost relaxed. Now she seemed troubled again.

"Why do you need money to go to work?" he asked quietly. "It's usually the other way around. Most people go to work to get money."

She didn't look at him. "I have to—finish some courses. Then be—trained and stuff. For this particular salon. That's their policy. I train for six months. And I don't get paid while I learn. You can't have everything."

"I see," he said, but he didn't. He had seen plenty of makeup artists in his time, and she was good, very good. Why would a woman with her looks and talent settle for so little?

"If makeup's your game," he asked carefully, "why not stay in Manhattan? Or go to Hollywood? Work in TV? Or the movies?"

"After this, I don't want to have anything to do with show business," she said passionately, staring out at the desert horizon. "I *hate* it."

"Why?" he asked. He could see the tension in her body.

"I don't want to talk about it," she said. She turned toward him again, her face a mask of coolness. "After all—*you're* from Hollywood. Of course, you'd laugh at Gooseburg, New Jersey. Tell me about your glorious career instead. How'd you hurt your rib? Defying death?"

Very good, Gil thought wryly. *She dropped her guard for a few seconds, but she's recovered—and wants me on the defensive instead. She's had practice keeping people at a distance. A lot of practice.*

He answered as nonchalantly as possible. "How'd I hurt my rib? Falling down a mountain."

"You should be more careful."

"I am careful. I'm the most careful man you'll ever meet. Accidents happen."

"And the cut on your side?" He sensed that she was taking his measure as minutely as he was taking hers.

"A horse kicked me. We took a fall on a gag."

"A gag?"

"A stunt. A gag's a stunt."

"Another accident?" she asked, disdain in her voice.

"Yes. It's unusual, two that close. It's been one of those shoots, that's all."

"It's a dangerous job."

"I like it."

"I wouldn't." She turned to the window again, hugging herself as if she was cold.

He had an urge to step up behind her, to put his hands on her shoulders, to try to draw some of the tension out of her.

He was tense, and it was because of her, the urges she awoke in him. He stood, but didn't go near her.

"You'd rather be safe?" he asked.

She didn't answer.

"Nobody's safe," he said in a low voice, thinking of Melly. "Not really. You never know what might happen next."

"You can," she said, squaring her shoulders. "Some people can. That's how I'll live. I'll always know what's going to happen next."

"No surprises?"

"I don't like surprises."

He watched the afternoon light dance on her blond hair. "Is that how you'd like everything? Settled—predictable?"

"Why not?" She gave the careless shrug that he was beginning to find irritating.

"It'd be boring."

"I wouldn't mind."

"You'd never be Caressa again?"

"No."

"You'd just be yourself?"

She gave another of her maddening shrugs. He realized he had moved, almost without volition, so that he was near her again, very near. If he but raised his hand, he could touch her, feel the soft warmth of her body through the oversize shirt. He frowned at the unwanted impulse.

"You told me there *was* no real you," he said, an edge coming into his tone. "And I shouldn't bother looking for one. Is that true?"

She seemed to flinch at the closeness of his voice and took a hasty step away, then turned toward him again. Worry and confusion flickered in her blue gaze. "Yes," she said in a voice that would have sounded tough if he hadn't seen the expression in her eyes. "I'm nobody to bother about.

You've been—I guess *kind* is the word. I appreciate it. But all this is *wearing,* and I think I'd like to be alone."

Without thinking, Gil reached for her, but she eluded him, stepping toward the door to her room. She looked at his outstretched hand with something akin to real alarm.

But she forced her mouth into a restrained smile. "I guess I'll see you again soon enough," she said. "Right?"

"Right," he agreed, his voice low. "When we go to buy a marriage license."

"Right," she said, her smile disappearing. She turned and entered her bedroom, leaving him staring after her. He heard the click of her lock, definite as an official announcement—*stay away from me.*

WHEN HE KNOCKED on her door a few hours later, Nikki was ready for him. She'd had time to rest, to gather her thoughts, to marshal her willpower. And, once more, she could hide behind Caressa's persona.

She wore the expensive custom jeans that Caressa favored, high-heeled boots, a white cashmere sweater and a red suede jacket. She had loosened her hair but covered most of it with a black silk scarf tied under the chin.

Nikki wore wraparound sunglasses, and Gil looked slightly startled when he saw her. She hoped she resembled Caressa attempting to go unnoticed. It was a difficult task, but she'd redone her makeup, and she thought she'd succeeded.

Gil, she guessed, was relying on his sunglasses and the upturned collar of his black leather jacket for camouflage.

He stared down at her, then shook his head. "That's the fourth face I've seen on you today. The only one I've really liked is your own."

She ignored his two-edged compliment. When she'd agreed to the assignment, she hadn't allowed herself to think much about the stuntman. Now she found herself uncomfortably conscious of him all the time and didn't like it. Evelyn wouldn't like it, either. Nikki had expressly promised Evelyn to be careful of this man.

"The question is," Nikki said loftily, "do I look like her? I mean do I look like her when she's trying *not* to look like herself?"

"Yes. You're scary, you know that?" he said, opening the door into the foyer. "You keep changing—like a chameleon."

She stepped into the spacious entry area. "I'm supposed to keep changing," she said, adjusting her sunglasses. "It's my job. It's yours, too."

Gil had exchanged his worn jeans for a pair of tailored black ones. He wore a gray silk shirt and the black leather jacket with its turned up collar. His dark hair was brushed into place with military precision. Only the closest observer would have noticed that his lips were thin in comparison to Chandler's almost fleshy ones.

"My job isn't to look like other people," he said. "My job is action work. Looking like somebody is incidental."

"It's hardly incidental," she said stubbornly. "If you couldn't pass for Chandler, you couldn't do his stunts. You're a chameleon yourself."

Gil's shoulders moved restlessly inside the leather jacket. He pressed the gold button to open the private elevator. With a soft sigh, the mirrored doors slid open.

"Come on," he said without enthusiasm. "Let's go get a marriage license."

NIKKI FELT TENSE while they were in the bureau, but they got the license without incident. More than one person seemed to recognize them, and a few actually gaped as their two bodyguards escorted them to the limousine.

She nearly collapsed with relief when they got into the car. She let out an enormous sigh. Gil, beside her, put a protective arm around her and for the moment she was too exhausted not to be grateful.

"Fine," he whispered in her ear. "Just great." He gave her shoulders an encouraging squeeze. Nikki knew she shouldn't like his embrace as much as she did, but was too wrung out to protest. She turned her face away and stared out the window to distract herself.

The streets were busy, the walks crowded, and a small knot of people had formed on the opposite sidewalk, watching them.

For a moment, through the smoky glass, Nikki's gaze met a pair of eyes that gave her an unpleasant shock. Among the faces in the crowd was one that stood out. A pale and flaccid man stared toward her with the most extraordinarily pale eyes she had ever seen. Blue-white, they seemed almost inhuman.

She froze because the man's gaze seemed riveted fanatically upon her own. It took her a moment to realize that he could not see her through the one-way window. It was simply the car that he stared at with such peculiar avidity.

Then, as the limousine pulled into the street, the man reached into the pocket of his khaki jacket, as if touching some object within. An odd smile crossed his face. Then he faded into the crowd so completely it was as if he'd never been there and Nikki had only imagined him. Her muscles tautened.

"What's wrong?" Gil said in her ear. They kept their voices down because the driver was a stranger, and they suspected he might eavesdrop.

"That man," Nikki breathed, drawing nearer to Gil without realizing it. "He was right over there. The way he looked at us—there was something about him, about his eyes. They were the palest eyes I've ever seen."

"Where?" Gil demanded, his grip on Nikki tightening.

"He disappeared into the crowd, just vanished," Nikki whispered. "I can't see him any more."

The larger of the two bodyguards, a red-haired man named Waldo, shook his head impassively. "Don't worry," he said with solemn assurance. "People are supposed to stare at you. You're safe. That's why we're here."

The other bodyguard frowned. He was a black man named Moses, and his face grew thoughtful. "Pale eyes? It could have been our friend. *We* should have seen him if it was. What else did you notice?" he asked Nikki.

"He was pale all over," she said. "Pale skin, fair hair, like blond going gray. A pasty face. He had a khaki jacket. It was faded."

"Who's your friend?" Gil demanded, as if he sensed trouble.

"Impossible," Waldo scoffed. "I would have noticed him. We don't even know if he's here."

"He could be," Moses argued. "This rumor's been out for *weeks,* man. We've been trying to convince everybody she'd be here now. It doesn't take Sherlock Holmes to figure she could go to the license bureau today."

"Impossible," Waldo repeated stolidly. He gave Nikki a patronizing smile. "Look—he didn't *do* anything, did he? He didn't do anything *menacing,* did he?"

Nikki gave a helpless shrug. Waldo's question and his condescending smile put her off balance. It was true the man had done nothing threatening. He'd only stared at them, then smiled his odd smile. In a moment of exhaustion, had she simply imagined he was sinister? He was gone now, so she might never be certain.

She shook her head, a gesture that said she could not know if the man was really dangerous.

"I don't know," Moses said, his brow furrowing more deeply. "That guy always seems to know—"

Waldo elbowed him discreetly, but Nikki felt Gil's body tense. "What guy?" Gil demanded in a low voice.

"It's nothing," Waldo said with a wave of his thick hand. "He's a nut case. He always seems to know where she is. He'll show up. He'll write. Or try to phone. But he's nothing to worry about. He never makes threats."

"That's true," Moses agreed, cocking a dark eyebrow. "He's never made a threat. If he did, we could get a restraining order put on him—keep him away. But he's never threatened. We don't know what goes on in his head."

"Aw," Waldo said with a disgusted growl, "it couldn't be him. This soon? He was in New York yesterday. At the license bureau already? Waiting for us? He'd have to be Superman or something." He gave Moses a challenging look.

Moses simply shrugged.

Gil's arm tightened around Nikki. He acted as if he intended to keep her that way, safe within the shelter of his arm, until they were alone again.

Her conscience gave her an uncomfortable twinge. Was he being merely supportive? Or seductive? For the life of her, she couldn't tell. All she knew, tired as she was, was that she didn't want to look to him for anything—strength, comfort, safety or pleasure of any kind.

She set her jaw and tensed her muscles. He seemed to sense her rising uneasiness. To her alarm, he bent his head and his lips brushed her cheek, lingeringly, teasingly, as if promising greater pleasures to come. "Hey—remember," he whispered, "we're in love. Smile."

She saw Moses look away discreetly and Waldo fight back a smirk. She wanted to draw away but forced herself not to, only because she didn't know whether the chauffeur was a spy.

"There, there," Gil whispered in her ear. "Relax. We'll take care of you."

I take care of myself, Nikki thought unhappily. *Nobody takes care of me except me. And it's time I show this man just that.*

As soon as they reached the hotel and were in the privacy of the elevator, Nikki gave him the coldest look she could.

"What's the matter?" he asked, frowning.

"I hate it when you touch me," she said, just as coldly. But in her heart, she knew it was a lie.

CHAPTER SIX

NIKKI LOCKED HERSELF IN the lavishness of the peacock bedroom, hung up her jacket and kicked off her boots.

She took off the black silk scarf and sunglasses. After washing her face, she shook out her hair, brushing it until it crackled. Finally she took a bath in the big gold tub that was also decorated with jeweled peacocks. At last she felt clean and almost as if she owned herself again.

Then she put the oversize shirt on and collapsed across the iridescent silks of the bed. Troubling images flickered through her mind, but soon she slept. The same images pursued her in her nightmares.

She dreamed a terrible, tangled dream of Rhonda and her low-life boyfriends. She was haunted by Rhonda's tired desperate face and Rhonda's ruined voice.

Then somehow, with the illogic of dreams, she *became* Rhonda. The cruel man she was clinging to became Gil. She was begging him, pleading with him, "Will you love me? Will you take care of me? Will you? Will you?"

The Gil of her dream looked down in contempt, his mouth twisted in a smile. Then he pushed her hands away, laughed, turned his back and walked off. "Wait!" she cried after him. "Please wait!" But there was no one there. She stood alone in a field of ashes under a somber sky.

Nikki awoke with a start. For a moment she lay looking at the intricate embroidery of the canopy, her heart drumming. Then she realized it was not just the dream that had awakened her but a noise, an irregular rapping.

What? she wondered in confusion. Someone was knocking at the door. Was it Gil, the cruel man in her dream?

Still groggy, she rose and went to the door. "What? Who is it? What do you want?"

For a moment her only answer was silence. Then she heard Gil's somewhat sarcastic voice. "I've got two orders of pasta primavera out here—Moses smuggled it up. If you want real food come get it. We've got an hour till show time."

He put ironic emphasis on the words *show time.* Nikki winced, remembering how soon she would again be in his arms. Her spirits plummeted even lower when she remembered her nightmare of becoming Rhonda, poor, helpless Rhonda.

"I'm not hungry," she said haughtily. Her stomach gave a growl of betrayal.

"You're lying," Gil said with disgust. "Fine. I won't beg you. I'll set it by the door. Starve. Tough. As if I give a damn."

Nikki clenched her fists. She'd just been repelled by her nightmare of being dependent on this man. Now he was at her door, offering to take care of her needs, tempting her.

"I'm not hungry," she repeated.

She thought she heard him swear. There were footsteps, a clinking sound, footsteps again, then more clinking.

"There," Gil growled. "It's in front of your door. It was nice of Moses to go to the trouble. He isn't paid to fetch and carry. If this is how you thank him, fine. Keep to yourself."

She heard his footsteps move away once more. She waited for what seemed a long time. Her stomach growled again, more hungrily. Beneath the door wafted the aroma of hot food steaming in rich sauce. It smelled so delicious that she could barely stand it.

The tinkle of silverware played from somewhere on the other side of the door. Gil was sitting down, enjoying himself, eating, while she stood there starving because of her pride and stubbornness.

Oh, heavens, it's only food. I could have gotten it myself, Nikki thought. *Besides, he's right. If Moses took the trouble to bring it, I shouldn't waste it.*

Weakening, she unlocked the door and inched it open. On the white carpet rested a gold enameled tray. On the tray was the gold-covered dish from which the mouth-watering odor floated. A cut-glass plate held a green salad drenched in dressing, a smaller, matching plate offered antipasto, and a single white rose bloomed from a gold bud vase.

She bent and reached for the tray almost furtively, her stomach growling for the third time. At the same moment, she glanced around the room. A powerful sensation jolted through her when Gil's black eyes met hers.

He sat in one of the dining chairs at a table covered with a snowy white cloth. The set of his dark eyebrows gave him a casually rakish look.

One corner of his mouth snaked up in mockery, and he smiled unpleasantly. He saluted her with his coffee cup. "If it isn't Miss Congeniality. She's hungry, after all. Eat hearty, Miss Congeniality. And always stay as sweet as you are."

A blush burned Nikki's cheekbones. She was uncomfortably aware that, for the second time that day, he had seen her without her makeup. "It's a shame to waste food, that's all," she said, gripping the tray and rising. "Thank Moses for me."

"Anything I can do to satisfy your needs," he said. He favored her with another insincere smile and another salute with his coffee cup.

She turned away with as much dignity as she could, bearing the tray into her room, then went to shut the door. The lock fell into place with an extraordinarily loud click. The sound signified, with rude finality, that she was shutting herself in, him out.

GIL STARED at the locked door that separated him from
Nikki. Although the food before him was delicate and delicious, he barely tasted it. He frowned, twin lines deepen-
ing between his brows.

The image of her naked face still floated in his mind. It
was illogical, it was unlike him, but whenever he saw her real
face, he was reminded of a flower. Not a voluptuous and
pampered hothouse flower. Not a well-bred and tended
blossom from a garden. No, she reminded him of a wild
flower, as if she had managed to grow up beautiful in a place
that was secret, untamed, harsh.

Before coming to Vegas in this crazy masquerade, he had
imagined half a dozen unpleasant scenarios with the girl.
But she fit none of them.

When he looked on her unadorned face, or when he held
her and kissed her, something deep within him threatened
to leap out of control. He hadn't felt this way since Melly.
Why? It was more than the woman's physical beauty, for he
had known women far more glamorous. It was not her personality, for it was mercurial, skittish, fragmented by par-
adox.

For want of a better word, he wondered if he was intrigued by her *character.* She combined fragility with
toughness. She seemed full of needs, but so independent
that she hated herself when she accepted help.

Above all, he sensed that behind her aloofness, her
scornful little smile, she had secrets, many of them. He intended to find out what they were. Knowledge was power.
Once he knew her, he would understand her, the mystery
would vanish, and he would be free of the unwanted spell
she cast.

The sooner the better. What use did he have for a kid
whose highest ambition was to sell face paint in Gooseburg, New Jersey? Who hated show business and whose
goal was to make life safe and boring?

He wanted her out of his system. Somehow she angered him and made him angry at himself, as well. His unwilling interest in her had to stop. He would stop it whatever way he could.

ROACH HAD SPECIFIED what Nikki was to wear at each appearance. Tonight she donned form-fitting slacks of white velvet and a hip-length white sweater embroidered with gold threads. Rhinestone bracelets weighted both her wrists.

Her blond hair was to be worn full and wavy, not crimped, and it looked right to her. Her makeup was perfect. That was her exterior. Fine. Within, she felt far from fine. She struggled to create and keep a safe psychological distance between herself and Gil.

She could not allow herself to think of him as a man, not even as a human being. He was a means to an end, that was all. He was her ticket out of New York and into a sane, normal life. *Normal,* she told herself repeatedly. *Normal. Like everybody else.*

At last, taking a deep breath, she decided she was ready. But when Gil's knock rattled the door, her calm fell apart, and the pieces of it flew off, disappearing in a dozen different directions.

Feeling tremulous, she nevertheless drew herself up tall when she swung open the door. "Yes?" she said. "Is it time?"

"It's time." Gil's tone vibrated with aggravation. "Lord, I can't get used to this." He swore softly.

He hadn't changed his clothes but had added a heavy mohair sweater of pale blue over his shirt. Nikki's heart took another of its unauthorized leaps.

The thickness of the sweater made his shoulders seem even broader and his hips, by contrast, leaner. Its color emphasized the bronzed tan of his angular face, the darkness of his eyes.

"You can't get used to what?" Nikki was confused not only by his words but by her reaction to his presence.

"The way you change." Gil cast her a brief, disgusted glance. "An hour ago, your door opened, and I saw a girl with freckles and a beautiful pink mouth trying to sneak pasta into her room. Now she's gone. Instead, out walks a blond bombshell—nuclear strength. I get the feeling there might be twenty women in that bedroom, not just one."

Nikki willed her pulse to slow. It refused to obey. "Don't be silly," she said, walking to the nearest mirror to inspect her makeup. "You're in movies. They're illusion, too. You should be used to it."

"I am. In the movies. Not in my life."

He had followed her and stood looking over her shoulder at their reflected images. In the mirror, her eyes met his, then wavered and looked away. She pretended to be interested in adjusting a strand of hair.

"I keep reminding myself that you're really in there," he said, his deep voice soft. "That you're you, not her."

"Why bother?" Nikki said flippantly. She moved because his closeness made her nervous, but he moved with her. His nearness tingled like electricity up and down her spine.

"Why bother?" His voice was sardonic. "Because I like to know true from false. Because I like to know what I'm dealing with—and whom."

"*Whom?*" Nikki mimicked with a brittle smile. "Aren't you grand? I could never figure out when to say *whom*. Is that the way to use it? Or are you just showing off—pretending to know?"

"My God," he said between his teeth. "You want to pick on my *grammar?* You're impossible. Yeah, I know when to use it. My mother taught English. I never split an infinitive, either. I'm a real marvel."

Nikki turned to him, her back to the sliding doors that opened onto the veranda. She raised her chin. "An English teacher. My. Educated. You must have been very, very well brought up. I'm impressed. My, my."

"Brought up better than I wanted to be. My father was a minister."

Nikki searched his face to see if he was joking. But his expression was stern, unyielding. Once more she sensed that he was standing too close, but she could back away no farther. Her shoulder blades already touched the drapes that hid the veranda doors.

"A minister," she repeated, her tone lightly derisive. "Oh, *wow*. You *were* well brought up. But you ended up in Hollywood. What are you—the black sheep of the family?"

"For a while," he muttered. "They've accepted it. What about you? Your parents? What kind of family sheep are you? Black? White? Lost? Or merely stray?"

Nikki's smile died. "I'm no kind of family sheep. There isn't any family. They were entertainers. Or tried to be." She ducked her head so she wouldn't have to meet his intent gaze any longer. "Look—we should go outside. Get this thing over with. Oh, I'm so *tired* of pretending to be something I'm not."

She turned and pushed back the drapes, then tried to open the sliding door, struggling with the lock. It resisted her. She struggled harder, dreading the scene they were about to play, wanting to be done with it.

"Let me," Gil said in his low voice, moving behind her. "And calm down. We're supposed to go out there like lovers. You don't bolt out alone."

He slipped one arm around her waist and drew her near him smoothly, irresistibly. Nikki tensed. "Steady," he said in her ear. Resting his chin on her shoulder, he reached his free arm around her and clicked open the lock. "There," he said softly as he pushed the drape out of their way. The warmth of his breath fluttered provocatively against her throat. "Now, we take it slow and easy. Very slow. Very easy."

Keeping his arm around her, he slid the door open. The coolness of the desert night washed over Nikki in a chilly wave. She shivered slightly. Gil's arm tightened around her waist. "Go over to the waterfall," he said in her ear, then kissed the corner of her jaw. His lips, in the cool darkness, were so warm that the rest of her body felt cold.

Another shiver rippled through her. The veranda was huge, taking up much of the highest section of the hotel's roof. Paved with white flagstones, the area was landscaped with palms, cacti, exotic evergreens and potted plants.

The heated water in the swimming pool, lit from beneath, swayed and twinkled, giving off ghostly wisps of steam. At the pool's far end the artificial waterfall tumbled down its miniature man-made mountain, sparkling and gurgling. It, as well as the pool's edge, was lit by small colored spotlights, hidden in the foliage. Plants and trees were clustered thickly around the waterfall.

"Who stays in this place?" Nikki breathed. "Princes and sheikhs?"

"Precisely. An Arabian prince. A very liberated Arabian prince. He leased it for a hundred years. He's loaned it to Caressa." His arm tightened around her. "Over here."

He guided her toward a grove of artfully twisted pines. "Let's not make it easy on them, over in the Silverado. Let's stay out of clear sight for a while—make it seem natural."

Nikki forced herself to smile. "You said *them*. Is more than one photographer over there now?" She nodded toward the Silverado.

"Right," he answered, steering her into the shadows of a grove of cedars. "At least two more checked in this afternoon. The first one's been here since Sunday, just in case we showed up early. Roach is watching from over there, too. He rented a room. I think he's got his own photographer, just in case nobody else comes up with a decent picture. Also, he wants to see how well we do.''

Nikki felt a stab of repugnance. ''This is madness,'' she said as they moved into the darkest part of the grove. The miniature waterfall hissed and roared, and the sharp scent of chlorine danced on the air, mingling with the tang of pines.

Beyond the veranda, she could see the lights of hundreds of other hotels, nightclubs and casinos, the silent winking and blinking rainbow of Vegas's kingdom of neon.

Gil stopped moving, and so did Nikki. She began to disengage herself from his embrace, but he held her fast. ''Shh,'' he cautioned. ''Stay close. They can't see much of us from where they are, but they *can* see us. Especially with you all in white.''

There was a small bench of pale marble facing the waterfall through the pines. The colored light fell through the branches in soft, irregular patches.

''Sit,'' Gil said, releasing her. ''You're nervous again, aren't you?''

Nikki sank to the bench, grateful to be even partially hidden. ''Who wouldn't be? All these people spying—even Roach. Good grief. Caressa and Chandler, how do they stand it? Living like this? Cooped up, hiding from the press? Being cannibalized by the public? How do they stay sane?''

He sat beside her, his face shadowy in the faint light. ''It's the price you pay for being rich and famous. It's like a bargain with the devil.''

''What do you mean?'' His words prickled her uncomfortably. She wondered if she had bargained with the devil by signing Roach's contract.

''They have wealth—power,'' he said. ''But they sign away their place in the human community. Whom can they trust? Who'll ever like them for themselves? Or be loyal to them out of friendship, not for money? They stop being people. They become commodities."

"It sounds terrible," Nikki said, gazing at the empty sky. It was a dull and depthless black, lit by neither moon nor stars.

"For the really famous, everything's done in front of a camera. The whole world watches while they fall in love, marry, divorce. They can't even have a nervous breakdown or die alone. The press is always there, turning everything into news."

"It *is* terrible," Nikki said, "I'd hate it."

"Me, too."

"Why does anybody want it?" she asked, turning to look at the rush of the artificial waterfall lit by its colored lights.

"You tell me." He reached over and picked up her hand, lacing his fingers through hers, then setting their linked hands on the hardness of his thigh.

Nikki's breath deserted her at his unexpected touch. Her smooth hand felt both seared and chilled by the contact with his rougher one. "Don't—" she began to say, although she did not try to draw away.

"Shh," he said, laying his finger against her lips. "You're uneasy again. Don't be afraid when I touch you. It means nothing. We have to do this. Get used to it. Get comfortable with it."

"I can't."

"You can." He drew his finger slowly across the softness of her lower lip, then, even more slowly, traced the curve of the upper. "Let me touch you. Learn to touch me. This can't work if we don't trust each other. So touch me. And talk to me. Get used to it."

His finger left the tingling curve of her mouth and his hand moved to clasp her free one gently. He carried her hand to his face and held it against his angular cheek. His face felt hard and blood warm beneath her cool fingertips.

"That's right," he said so low it was almost a whisper. "Just touch me. I'll help you." He kept his hand upon hers so that her fingertips began to grow reluctantly familiar with the austere curve of his cheekbone.

Nikki's breath caught in her throat, and her heart shook against her ribs. He moved her hand slightly so that he could kiss her, lingeringly, on the palm.

The kiss sent tremors racing down her spine that both warmed and weakened her. When at last he moved his lips away from her palm, his touch still burned there, as if she held a star, live and glowing, in her hand.

"Now," he said softly, "I asked you to tell me. If the price is so high, why does anybody want the burden of it, fame, fortune?" He gave a sarcastic twist to the last words.

"I—I..." She stammered, her hand still throbbing from his kiss. "I think they believe it will make them whole." She thought of Rhonda, who had thought only love or stardom could make her complete.

He guided her hand to his shoulder, clasping it there tightly so that her hand shaped itself to its hardness. "Make them whole? Interesting. But puzzling. What do you mean? Tell me. While we touch each other."

His hand left hers resting, hesitant and light, on his shoulder, like a bird that might fly away at any moment. Gently, he traced the curve of her jawline.

"How?" he repeated in his low voice. "How do they think it makes them whole? Tell me."

Nikki's brain raced. He was only trying to prepare her for what they must soon do before the cameras—wasn't he? He was only trying to make her more comfortable—wasn't he? But if he was trying to calm her, why did she feel so exhilarated *and* so frightened?

"Some people," she said, trying to control her warring emotions, "some people don't feel whole. They need something to complete themselves—" she thought again of Rhonda "—or they feel they aren't worth anything. Maybe it's being famous. Or—rich. Or powerful, too. They don't feel significant without those things. Maybe they don't even feel *alive* without them."

He tipped her chin so that she had to gaze at his shadowed face. "You do understand it. But you don't need those things. Not you."

Her combating sensations tore at her. She wanted to rebel against what his touch did to her; she wanted to surrender to it. His combination of power and gentleness enthralled her against her will, but she had to remember how different, how alien this man was from her.

"No," she said tautly. "I don't. But you must need them—or something worse. Or you wouldn't do what you do. You need danger. You need to take chances."

He was silent a moment. His hand against her face went still, as if what she said had taken him aback.

"Once I did," he said at last. "That's changed. What I need now is to go forward, go farther."

"What?" Nikki asked fliply. "More danger? Bigger chances?" She tossed her head to free herself from his touch, but she kept her hand on his shoulder, more to keep him at a distance than to draw him nearer.

"No," he said, leaning nearer anyway, his hand settling possessively on her arm. "Bigger challenges, that's all. To be the guy calling the shots, not doing them. Why so tense, Nikki? What does it matter what I do or want to do?"

"It doesn't," she answered, feeling even more strained. "I don't care at all. Look—can't we get out there where they can see us and take their stupid pictures and get this over with?"

She tried to wriggle away, but both his hands were on her upper arms now, holding her fast. "Steady, Nikki. I want you calm, remember?"

"I *am* calm," she lied.

"You're not." His hands moved up and down her arms, a motion that soothed and excited her. "I can feel it even through this damned sweater. Your muscles are knots."

"Because I want to be *done* with this," she protested, shaking her head. "Because I *hate* this."

He stood, drawing her up with him. She felt dwarfed by his height, threatened by his nearness. Something subtle in his manner changed, although she could not say what it was. He stared at her, and she glared back.

His voice was harsh when he spoke. "There's no use hating it. It's what you have to do to get to New Jersey. It's what I have to do to direct. I don't like it, either, but that's the way it is."

"Direct?" Nikki said, blinking at him in surprise. "You mean that's what you get out of this deal? You get to *direct?*" She gave a short laugh. "Isn't that the biggest cliché in Hollywood? Everybody wants to *direct?*"

His hands gripped her arms more tightly. "Don't hide behind wisecracks, Nikki. We can't afford to be enemies. Too much is at stake. For both of us."

She knew she had been defensive and was ashamed of herself. "I'm sorry," she said in true frustration. "I just meant—"

"It doesn't matter what you meant. So what if I dream big and you dream small? We're here to make those dreams real. We've got a job to do. Let's be professional." His tone softened. "Look. Like it or not, we're a team. I depend on you. And you depend on me."

Nikki looked away from him, disturbed. Through the pine branches she watched the imitation waterfall cascading down its imitation rocks, bathed in artificial light. "We're a team," he repeated. "All I want is for you to trust me and feel comfortable with me, all right?"

She nodded, still not looking at him, although she was afraid to trust him and was afraid she'd never feel comfortable with him.

"Are you ready?" he asked, drawing her nearer to him.

A lump had formed in her throat that wouldn't go away. She swallowed. "I'm ready."

"We're going to walk out there, to the left, the other side of the waterfall. I'll keep my arm around you. We'll go as far as that bed of ornamental cacti. The light's strong enough there that they should see our faces, but not too well. They should have a fairly clear shot of us."

Nikki nodded. She had the sudden nervous urge to bite her lip, but resisted for fear it would mar her makeup.

He bent closer. "When we get there, I'll take you in my arms—like this." His hands clasped her waist, pulling her against his body, slowly, sensuously. Nikki felt the hard length of his thighs against hers, the pressure of his chest against her yielding breasts.

"Then," he said, his voice low, "I'll kiss you—be sure and kiss me back. About two minutes worth. I'll time it. All right?"

"All right," she said weakly.

"Now," he whispered, "out there, it's going to be for Caressa and Chandler and Roach and the photographers. But now, here—this one is for us."

His lips began to descend toward hers.

"Us?" Nikki breathed.

But she could say no more. His mouth took hers.

CHAPTER SEVEN

IN THE COOL DESERT NIGHT, Nikki's private world reeled dizzily out of control. She wanted Gil to kiss her, perhaps forever. She didn't want him to kiss her, not ever, not now.

Although she raised her hands to push him away, instead her fingers rested, hesitant, reluctant, against his sweatered chest.

Her lips parted to cry out in protest, but no sound came. Instead, he kissed her more deeply, the warmth of his mouth canceling the chill of the dark breeze. His lips were sure, expert, and his touch somehow combined gentleness with irresistible strength. And although this intimacy alarmed her, it also overwhelmed her with yearning.

Nikki had been kissed before, but not with gentleness. Men had used their strength to try to satisfy themselves, but none had ever tried to give her pleasure. This was exactly what Gil seemed determined to do, to teach her the sweetest secrets of touch.

When his mouth moved against hers, it was as if he was speaking without words. *This can be nice, Nikki. It can be good. It can be right. It can be like this.*

He wound one arm around her waist, drawing her to him more intimately. His other hand moved to her throat, then under the thick fall of her hair to her nape. Nikki shivered, but not from cold, for she no longer felt the cold.

"Don't shudder," he whispered against her lips. "And don't fight me. We're a team, Nikki. I trust you, and you can trust me. Show you trust me. Kiss me back."

The breeze rose, and she shivered again. His thumb traced the line of her jaw, and she stared at him, his face shadowy in the starless night. She knew she should draw back, that she should rebuke him. But she said nothing, and she stayed within the circle of his arms.

"Show me," he breathed. "That you trust me. Kiss me. Just once without an audience."

Her hands still rested against the softness of his sweater. She could feel the muscle and warmth of his body and the steady drumming of his heart beneath her fingertips.

Beyond them, the waterfall tumbled, and from far below floated the sound of the ceaseless Vegas traffic. But Nikki heard nothing except the thudding of her own heart. Gently his hand moved to frame her jaw. She tried, falteringly, to turn her face away from him, but he would not let her.

"Nikki," he said, his breath warm on her lips, "kiss me." His tone was low, encouraging, even kindly.

She studied the planes of his shadowed face for the space of three heartbeats. Each beat tightened the knot in her throat. Shivering again, she raised herself on tiptoe.

Slowly, hesitantly, her lips touched his. He made no move to force her closer or increase the pressure of the kiss. Her mouth trembled, barely brushing his, and although she had the impulse to draw away immediately, she did not.

She found herself unable to kiss him more boldly, although she wanted to. Yet neither could she pull away from him, although, paradoxically, she wanted that, as well.

Instead she kept her lips shyly touching his, as if spellbound and unable to do otherwise. Her senses whirled, tremulous. She thought she felt his heart quicken beneath her fingertips. His hand against her face had gone perfectly still, as if he wished to make no move to startle her.

"Oh," she breathed, sighing the word without volition. The sound startled and shamed her, and she drew back from him, staring at the lights that fell through the pine branches.

For a moment his hand lingered on her face, but when she refused to look at him, she felt it fall away.

He took her by the hand. "Come on," he said softly. "Let's go pretend to be in love."

Nikki nodded curtly, dreading the scene to come. She was already emotionally exhausted, torn in too many directions. She tossed her head and tried to put on her most aloof air. "Now I'm supposed to drive you mad with passion? It's not my usual bent. As you can tell."

He led her toward the section of veranda wall nearest the Silverado. He squeezed her hand. "We won't go for mad passion. We'll just take it easy, all right?"

Nikki's brow creased with worry. "But Roach said—"

"Forget Roach," Gil said, draping his arm around her shoulder. "Just smile. Kind of snuggle up here. Lean on me. And smile. People in love don't have to climb all over each other all the time. Let's keep it natural."

Nikki snuggled into the crook of his arm, leaning her head against his shoulder. She managed a moody smile. "What do you know about it? Have you ever been in love?"

She felt his arm tense. He was silent a moment. "I was once." He sat on the wide wall, drawing her down beside him. "All right. Now we just talk. Every once in a while I'll kiss you. Keep looking into my eyes. As if we're in love."

Nikki looked into his eyes, which seemed as dark as the lightless sky behind him. She smiled, struggling to keep her voice light, careless. "Is this the director in you coming out? You map these scenes out in your mind?"

He leaned his forehead against hers, touched her lips with his forefinger. "I'm not that kind of director. Second unit is what I want. Nip at my finger playfully."

Nikki nipped, but he was quick. He began to stroke her lip again. "What's second unit?" she breathed.

"Action. I'd direct stunts. Rub noses with me."

Nikki rubbed her nose against his, surprised at the pleasant sensuality of the movement. He slipped his arms around her and nuzzled her ear.

"Don't jump. I'm going to put my hands under your sweater. Don't worry—I won't get too personal. Just keep smiling."

He rubbed noses with her again, and both shock and pleasure rippled up her spine when his hands moved under her sweater, warm against the cool flesh of her back.

When he smiled at her, she bit her lip, then tried to smile back.

"Such a little smile for me?" he asked. "You love me—remember? Come on. A bigger smile. Think of Roach in his underwear. Pink boxer shorts with green polka dots."

Nikki smiled more naturally.

"Good," he said. "Keep that smile. It's a beautiful smile. And keep your eyes on mine. Keep looking at me. In just that way."

She stared at him, smiling, not quite sure what look was in her eyes. But a troubled expression shone in his, in spite of the smile on his lips.

"That's it," he said, studying her face, "you've got it. You look like a woman in love. See? You're an actress after all." He stared at her for a long moment.

He looked more disturbed than before and shook his head, as if to clear it. "Put your arms around my neck. And when I kiss you, pretend to enjoy it. Make believe."

She swallowed and nodded, trying to keep her smile in place. Unaccountably, she felt tears sting her eyes and blinked them back as she raised her arms. She put her hands on the solid curve of his shoulders, then slid them to lock her fingers behind the back of his neck.

His eyes grew more disquieted when he saw the glint of her unshed tears. "Oh, God," he said softly. "Oh, God." He drew her to him and pressed her face against his shoulder, as if assuring her she was safe. He held her for a long moment, his heart beating as hard as hers.

Then he bent and kissed her, his hand still beneath her sweater, stroking her bare back. He didn't have to tell Nikki to kiss him back. This time she did so naturally, wanting to.

When at last he drew back, he was breathless, and so was she. He smoothed an errant strand of hair from her face, then stared at her parted lips. "Nikki." He shook his head, half-smiling, half-frowning. "Don't get *too* good at this. I'm only human. I think we'd better go inside."

She nodded solemnly. She reached over and gently rubbed a lipstick smear from his mouth. He caught her hand and kissed it. And this time when they looked at each other with desire, neither of them was pretending, and both of them knew it.

Inside, Gil poured a jigger of brandy and drank it straight. His face was taut. "Well," he said, from between his teeth, "that's done."

She stood near the draped doors to the veranda, nervous. She knew she should go to her room and close the door between them, but somehow she could not, not yet.

"When—when were you in love?" she asked, watching him.

He set his glass down and stared at it. "A couple of years ago." He poured another drink and turned to look at her. *What kind of woman is this?* he asked himself harshly. She stood there in her rhinestones and thousand-dollar sweater, looking as haughty as a high-fashion model and as ill at ease as a shy schoolgirl.

Tensely, she clenched her hands into fists at her sides, then unclenched them. "What happened to her? The woman you loved?"

Gil gritted his teeth and stared into his drink. "She died."

"I'm sorry."

"So am I."

"Were you—would you have married her?"

He tilted his glass and watched the brown sparkle of the liquor. "Yeah. I would have married her."

"Oh." Nikki moved to the couch and sat down. She ran her hand through her tousled hair and stared at her booted feet. "I'm sorry. I shouldn't have brought it up. It's just—"

She stopped, gave a helpless shrug, kept staring at her white boots.

"Just what?" he asked, frowning. She looked tired, confused, out of her element. At the same time she looked like a combination of show-biz princess and snow queen. And she also looked like a kid in too much makeup.

Nikki licked her lips. "It's just—if you'd married her, would you be here? Doing this? What we're doing?"

An odd question, he thought, one that made him feel slightly hollow, as if recovering from a punched stomach. It was a question that never would have been necessary if Melly were alive. Melly, he thought, with a wave of bitter guilt. Melly was the one he should be thinking of, not Nikki. Melly stayed alive—just a little—if he kept her in his mind all the time.

Melly was the one woman in the world he had truly loved. The only woman he would ever love. He had no business getting involved with this kid before him, this strange girl with whom he had nothing in common.

"No," he said shortly, looking at Nikki again, the lines of his face grim. "I wouldn't be here."

She nodded as if satisfied. "Not even if it meant a chance to direct—what'd you call it—the second unit? Action? You wouldn't be here even for that?"

"No. I'd have found another way. I wouldn't have left her to do something like this."

Nikki nodded again. She fiddled with one of her rhinestone bracelets. He didn't know what she was getting at or why he gave in to the impulse to explain to her, but he did. He took another sip of brandy.

"Her name was Melanie," he said, carefully keeping the emotion out of his voice. "She was from Monterey, the same as I am. She was a smart girl, a bright girl—studied history in college. Graduated with honors. But stunt work was what she loved. Like me. And that's what she ended up doing. And she was good." His voice softened and he shook his head in remembrance. "She was *good.*"

Nikki said nothing, still didn't look at him, but she seemed to be listening. Her expression had taken on an odd sadness. He took another drink.

"We met on a shoot. Rodeo movie. Not much of a movie. Nobody remembers it. But I do. The first time I saw her, she was on a big bay horse. Eighteen hands if it was an inch. Had a crazy look in its eyes. I said to her, 'How's a little thing like you going to handle a horse that big?' And she said, 'Just watch me, cowboy.'"

He shook his head at the memory, half-smiling to himself. He glanced at Nikki, whose golden head was still bent. Melly had been dark, flashing dark eyes, glossy dark hair, little and tomboyish with high color, a knowing look and a bold laugh. They had had almost everything in common, and she was as unlike this woman as possible, something he would do well to keep in mind.

His smile faded. "Then she started feeling—not so good. Which seemed crazy, because nobody ever looked healthier. But she kept feeling worse. And when she went to the doctors—" he paused, took another sip of his drink "—they knew something was wrong. Very wrong."

He took a deep breath, set his jaw. "They told me she had three, maybe four months to live. They said chemotherapy wouldn't help. The disease was too far gone."

He felt his body tense, remembering it, felt his face going wooden, as it always did when he tried to speak of it. "I had to tell her that. She said she wanted to hear the news from me, not some doctor. So I told her. That she had maybe four months. And she couldn't beat it."

A nerve twitched in his jaw. He looked around the room, at its infinity of mirrors. "She never flinched. But she didn't understand—not beat it? She didn't know how to fail at anything. She tried to smile, and she said, 'Just watch me, cowboy.'"

His hand tightened around his glass. "But she couldn't do it. She lasted exactly four months. We made them as good as we could. She was the most gallant woman I've ever known. There'll never be another one like her. Never."

He finished his brandy, set down the glass and pushed it away. He folded his arms. "That's it. That's the story. That's all."

Nikki looked up, her hands clenched between her knees. Once more he found it hard to read her tightly controlled face. He knew his own expression was just as contained.

She glanced around the room, as if searching for something to say. "Why is this room so different from mine?" she asked, and he was grateful for the change of subject. "It's like somebody took rooms from different countries and just glued them together."

He leaned against the silk-covered wall. "The prince wanted each room to represent a different time, place. The styles. The riches. This is French—neoclassic, Greek influence. Your room's mostly Indian—the heyday of the raj. Mine's Italian Renaissance. Do you want to look around? Ever see a kitchen done in ancient Egyptian? There's a microwave in a mummy case."

Nikki shook her head. She didn't want him to think she was trying to get invited to his room. Their situation forced them to be thrown into constant contact, and he had stirred feelings in her that she had not known existed.

Because she found him attractive, she had asked him, frankly, about the other woman. He had answered with equal frankness. He had loved Melanie, who was bright and educated and brave and gallant. "There'll never be another like her," he had said. The woman he'd loved was as unlike Nikki as possible. His words had felt like nails hammered into her heart.

He would never see anything in a person like her, who had to fight simply to read and who was proving far from fearless. It was just as well. She had no call to want any man, even one like Gil. Her job was not to want or need anybody, but to stand alone. She owed it to herself, she owed it to Evelyn, and she owed it, perhaps most of all, to Rhonda.

"Promise me," Rhonda had said at the end, "promise me you'll make something of yourself. Don't end up like me. Don't make my mistakes."

Suddenly the room seemed full of ghosts. Nikki tossed her head, sighed and lifted her heavy hair off her neck. Gil, she realized, was watching her with that same dark, troubled gaze as on the veranda.

"Oh," she said impatiently and rose from the couch. "I wish I could get out of here—just go out and walk. I feel like I'm in a fishbowl. And I've hardly even seen Las Vegas. Nothing but the airport."

She paced to the drapes, parted them slightly, then let them fall into place. "The airport had *aluminum* palm trees," she said, frowning. "And slot machines. People can step right off a plane and start gambling."

"I know."

"Here you can't even go outside without being spied on. I wonder if Roach would let me slip out alone—just for a while. Nobody would recognize me. I could make myself not look like her at all. Do you think he would?"

"No," Gil said, his expression unchanging.

Nikki faced him in exasperation. "Why? I'd take Waldo or Moses if either would go."

"No." Gil's voice was implacable.

"But *why?* We're through here for the night."

"We're getting married tomorrow, remember? He'll want you to get your beauty sleep."

"Married," she said with irony.

"Right."

"I won't be getting any sleep tonight, beauty or otherwise. I ought to be able to take a simple *walk.*"

He lowered one brow in a frown. "You can't. You're pretending to be her, and she's famous. She's a prisoner of that fame. So are you—for now."

Nikki sighed. She moved to the drapes again, but this time didn't bother to open them. "Why do you suppose they have metal palm trees in the airport? Instead of real ones? They aren't as pretty as real ones."

"It's Vegas. Not many things are real in Vegas."

She straightened her shoulders, tried once more to smooth her tumbled hair. "I see," she said, but she didn't. She would have liked to pull the drapes wide open, to look out on that wild, silent rainbow of lights that was Las Vegas at night, but knew she couldn't. People were watching, always watching.

"If you really want to go out, I'll take you," he said suddenly, his voice gruff.

Surprised, she turned to face him again. He hadn't changed his position. He leaned against the wall between two mirrors, his arms crossed, his face expressionless.

She eyed him warily, not sure what to think. "But you said that Roach—"

He shrugged. "The trick with Roach is not to ask for what you want. The trick is to *tell* him what you want. He'll be calling here any minute. I'll take care of it. Go change.

Put on something less conspicuous. And leave off the makeup. Or I won't take you out at all."

Nikki's heart began its manic, too swift beat again. "I *always* wear my makeup. I never go out—"

The phone rang, startling her. "Go on," Gil said, unsmiling, nodding toward her bedroom door.

She shrugged as if she didn't care, but moved toward her door, half-eager, half-reluctant to do as he said.

Hurriedly, she cleaned her face and brushed out her hair to its normal style, almost straight, barely waved. She hesitated a moment before the mirror. She could not stand the thought of going without makeup, her face bare for the world—and Gil—to see. She applied the slightest bit of lip gloss, the almost imperceptible stroke of mascara.

She searched the closet for the least conspicuous of Caressa's clothing. She put on the designer jeans and topped them with the oversize blue shirt. All of Caressa's jackets and sweaters seemed too expensive, too flamboyantly stylish. She decided she'd wear none. She'd rather be cold.

When she looked at her reflection, she looked young, inexperienced and not at all like Caressa. On impulse she took her hair and fastened it into two ponytails, one to hang over either shoulder. She looked even younger, even less like Caressa.

She returned to the sitting room, half expecting Gil to say that Roach wouldn't allow them out. But he stood near the front door, waiting, apparently impatient to go.

He wore the same faded jeans she'd seen him in earlier, the same worn flannel shirt, and a brown bomber pilot's jacket that looked as if he'd owned it for years. He also wore a pair of horn-rimmed glasses that gave him an unexpectedly serious, almost scholarly look.

She looked at him in surprise. Suddenly, except for his build and the cut of his hair, he looked nothing like Gavin

Chandler. The glasses had a strange effect; they emphasized both the strength and thoughtfulness of his face.

She stared in surprise. "I didn't know you wore glasses."

"Just for reading. But I figured with them, I don't look anything like Chandler. The world'll be blurry, that's all. Considering it's Vegas, that's fine with me."

He wore them for reading, Nikki thought, her heart shrinking. Of course, a man like him would read a lot. What would he think if knew she had trouble puzzling out even a simple note from Roach? Would he feel contempt? Or worse—pity?

"You didn't have trouble with Roach?" she asked as airily as she could.

"Roach has trouble with *me*. I don't play his game." He frowned at her. "Is that all you're going to wear? You'll freeze."

"I can't wear any of her heavy stuff. It all looks like it costs a fortune. I want to look—you know, natural."

He stared at her a long moment. "Here," he said, stripping off the bomber jacket. "Take this."

Nikki started to protest.

"Take it," he insisted gruffly. "I've got another one. Didn't they let you bring any of your clothes?"

Nikki shook her head and let him help her on with the jacket. It was odd slipping into it. The worn lining was still warm from his body, and the feel and scent of old leather was comfortable, almost familiar. It was as if he had owned the jacket so long, it was impregnated permanently with the feel of his body.

He went to his room and returned, shrugging into an old blue and white college letter jacket of wool and leather. He had an old blue baseball cap, as well, and had pulled it down at a rakish angle. Nikki smiled slightly. With the jacket, hat and glasses, he looked like a studious coach who taught math on the side—anything but an Australian movie star.

"You were a letter man?" she asked, almost shyly. Colleges and universities seemed like foreign countries to her, their traditions strange and exotic.

"Two years. Track and field. Come on. Moses is going to follow us. Discreetly. He's as restless as we are."

He ushered her into the foyer and pressed the elevator button. He glanced idly at their reflection in the mirrored doors. "You look like you should be taking a stroll on the college campus, not living in a sheikh's penthouse."

She shrugged, troubled. "What did you study? In college? Filmmaking?"

The elevator doors hummed open. He shook his head and guided her inside. "Engineering. It wasn't for me. I quit my junior year. I wanted to jump out of burning buildings and fall off horses. My brother stuck with it. He's a professor in Houston."

Nikki put her hands deep in the pockets of the jacket. She couldn't imagine anyone voluntarily dropping out of college, and the ease with which he accepted danger disturbed her. "I'd never quit college," she said pensively.

He, too, had his hands in his pockets. He stared ahead, not looking at her. "You follow your own star."

She nodded, as if reassuring herself. "And my star leads to Gooseburg, New Jersey."

He frowned. "If you want to go to college, go. You should have enough money after this. Sounds better than peddling makeup in Gooseburg."

She tilted her head, trying to look nonchalant. "Like you said, you follow your star."

The elevator stopped, and the doors opened. They stepped into the gloom of the basement. Moses waited for them in the shadows. He stared a moment, then nodded in recognition.

"Well, well," he said wryly. "Look at this. Real people. You're a pretty little lady, miss. Prettier than *her*."

Nikki thrust her fists deeper into the jacket pockets, embarrassed. "It's nice of you to come out with us."

He shook his head. "Nice has nothing to do with it. I feel like I've been playing gin rummy with Waldo for a hundred years. A man has got to *stretch* from time to time. You ready for the big day tomorrow?"

Nikki looked down at the concrete. "Ready as I'll ever be, I guess."

Moses grinned. "Roach says you're getting better at the noodling business. Said you were very convincing on the veranda tonight. Not what he had in mind—but convincing."

Nikki could think of nothing to say.

"Practice makes perfect," Gil muttered.

"So they say," Moses said. "Well, you two go your way. I'll stroll along behind you, just out of earshot. You can have your privacy—and I can have mine."

"Fine," Gil said. "We all need a vacation from this craziness." He took Nikki's arm and steered her toward the basement's side entrance.

"What will we see?" Nikki asked. "Do you know this town?"

He nodded. "What do you want to see? An erupting volcano? Knights on horseback? White tigers? A man floating on a cloud of fire? Mermaids? A car made of rhinestones? Clowns? Castles? A circus? Fire-eaters? A singing skeleton? A pool of sharks? Orchids? The *Titanic* sinking? Or would you rather drink champagne in the Grand Canyon?"

Nikki's imagination whirled. Was he teasing her, or could such wonders really be? The city was, after all, an even more fabled playground than New York. But erupting volcanos? Knights on horseback? "I want to see what it's *really* like," she said. "Don't tell me impossible things."

He opened the door to the night. "It's Vegas, Nikki," he said in his low voice. "Nobody knows what's real. And nothing's impossible here. Nothing."

CHAPTER EIGHT

GIL WAS RIGHT. In Las Vegas at night, nothing seemed real, yet nothing seemed impossible. Nikki was a New Yorker; she was therefore supposed to be worldly-wise, blasé and difficult to impress.

But Vegas was designed to dazzle, and dazzle it did. Las Vegas Boulevard, known simply as the Strip, offered the greatest light show in the world. Millions of colored bulbs and thousands of miles of rainbow neon pulsed blinked, shone and swirled.

Lights flickered and flared; they shimmered, gleamed, flashed, glowed and danced. Some were as steady as sunlight; others fluttered like fox fire, auroras and summer lightning.

"They're here," Gil said, gesturing at the wonderland of lights, "all the magic names. Aladdin, Excalibur, Caesar's Palace, the Mirage, the Sahara, the Dunes, the Sands."

Although it was nearly midnight, the sidewalks and streets were choked with crowds, and an almost desperate excitement pulsed in the air.

"What's *that* one?" Nikki asked as they turned a corner. She pointed at an enormous neon cowgirl shining against the dark sky. The cowgirl, scantily clad, seemed to sit on a heap of twinkling gold. Across the street, an even larger neon cowboy rose into the night, gesturing toward himself, as if inviting the cowgirl over to his spangled place.

"Glitter Gulch," Gil answered, nodding toward the cow-girl. "And there's the Golden Goose, the Golden Gate—and the Golden Nugget."

Nikki smiled at the Golden Goose, where a huge white goose sat in a nest of sparkling eggs. The goose wore a cowboy neckerchief, a Stetson and a beguiling grin to lure gamblers inside.

Nikki shook her head in wonder. How could people stay inside and gamble, she wondered, when they could be out here looking at this crazy, improbable spectacle?

She glanced behind them. Twelve paces to the rear, Moses strolled, seeming not to notice them. He glanced up at the winking forest of signs without emotion, as if he had seen them too often to be impressed.

"Want to see a show?" Gil asked. "We could catch a late one."

Nikki came back to herself. She suddenly felt cold and huddled more deeply into the leather jacket. "No, thanks."

"More stars perform here than anyplace on earth," Gil said. "And there are the stage spectaculars. Want to see an elephant fly? You can do it here, kid."

She shook her head. "I'm not interested. Thanks anyway. The elephant can fly without me."

He glanced at her. "You really mean it, don't you?"

She nodded, thinking of Rhonda. Rhonda had always wanted to play Vegas; it had been one of her dreams. *Don't make the same mistakes I did,* she had said.

"You've got it bad," Gil said, studying her somber face. "Why? Why so burned out?"

"I've had enough, that's all," Nikki said, squinting at a tall building at the end of the street. Gleaming tracks of light ran up its face, twenty stories high. She couldn't read its name because all the blinking signs became scrambled together, indecipherable to her.

"Are there really sharks here?" she asked, changing the subject. "In the desert? And white tigers? Were you teasing about the volcano erupting?"

"It erupts on a regular schedule. Over at the Mirage. They've built a whole volcanic island. Come on. I'll walk you over to Circus Circus. We can have a drink at the Hilton—they've got a quiet café. Then start back. Remember, tomorrow's the big day."

"I remember," she replied.

"Look at that," he muttered, nodding at one of the clubs across the street. "Essence of Vegas."

Nikki tried to follow his gaze, frowning. "Where? What do you mean?"

"Read it and weep," he said. "Double Jackpots Every Five Minutes, Free Slot Player's Glove. People play the slot machines so much they need a *glove*, for God's sake."

Nikki narrowed her eyes, perplexed by the thousands of signs.

"Over there," Gil said, "Lucky Lucy's."

"Oh." She stared at a sign with a neon cascade of coins and a bright set of messages gleaming out in red and gold, silver and black. "Oh. That."

Gil studied her face for a moment, then the black and silver sign. "You interested in any of that?" he asked.

"Double jackpots?" She gave him a cynical smile. "A free slot player's glove? No, thanks. I'm not a gambler."

He paused, staring at her so intently she looked away. "I forgot—you're the one who likes to play things safe. Not take chances."

"That's me," Nikki said. "Couldn't be more boring, could I?"

"What about down there?" Gil asked. "Doesn't that one tempt you? The one with the blue signs—Barbary Coast? That's a famous one—just a game of blackjack? I'll pay."

He gestured at a pair of tall blue signs, one with flashing gold letters, one with blazing white. "The Barbary Coast," he repeated, "you must have heard of it. Just one game of roulette, to say you've done it?"

"I'm not interested in the Barbary Coast," Nikki said, starting to walk again. "Which way to Circus Circus?"

"Back to the strip. Then south. I can't get over you in those ponytails. You *don't* belong in Las Vegas. Or New York. Where the devil do you belong?"

Nikki lifted one shoulder in a shrug. "I told you, New Jersey. I can't get used to you in those glasses, either. You look like you belong . . . in a library."

She could imagine him sitting in his own library, like a man in an advertisement. His long legs would be crossed comfortably, and he'd smoke a pipe. He'd study his book in a circle of lamplight. Behind him would be shelves of books, hundreds of them, with leather covers and gold titles. It was a world closed to her, and it depressed her deeply.

"There are worse places than a library," he said, casting her a sideways glance.

"It wasn't an insult," Nikki said, tossing her ponytails off her shoulder. "I just imagined you in a library, that's all. I don't know why. Do you have one?"

He pulled the bill of his hat lower over his eyes. "As a matter of fact, I do. I've got a house in the hills. With one room for books. Do you read much?"

Inwardly Nikki cringed, but she raised her chin rather haughtily, as if the question was beneath her. "Not enough time. Just what I had to read in English classes and stuff."

They turned onto the Strip. She ducked her head against the glitter of the lights. They were beginning to give her a headache.

"So what'd you like to read best?" Gil persisted.

She shook her head, wishing he'd drop the conversation. It made her nerves prickle skittishly.

"I don't know," she said, shrugging. "Poems, I guess."

"Really." He raised a speculative eyebrow. He slowed his pace and took her arm so that she, too, had to slow. He stopped, staring at her. At his touch, all her senses leaped, and she had the odd sensation that hummingbirds had been released in her stomach.

"Recite a poem for me, Nikki. Lord, my mother knew tons of them—she was something. Me, I never had a head for it."

Nikki's mouth went suddenly dry. She licked her lips and tried to swallow. She looked at him warily.

"Go on," he urged. "We're in a strange, enchanted city in the middle of the desert. It's night. We need a poem."

Nikki stared at the velvety darkness of the sky, where no stars shone. She knew a surprising number of poems by heart—she'd memorized them from tapes for classes. Much of her learning came from tapes. Perhaps because she had been thinking of Rhonda, one poem came irresistibly to mind.

She took a deep breath and began.

" 'Sigh no more, ladies, sigh no more,

"Men were deceivers ever—

"One foot in sea and one on shore,

"To one thing constant never.' "

She squared her shoulders as she finished and gave him a challenging look. "There. Satisfied?"

He raised an eyebrow. "Do you know who wrote that? Where it came from?"

She tilted her chin. "Shakespeare. A play. I don't know which one. I just learned the poem."

He drew her closer, started walking again. "You know others?"

"Yes."

"Recite me another. See if you can spout poetry all the way to Circus Circus."

Nikki laughed nervously, uncomfortable with his nearness. "Why?"

"I don't know. It makes me nostalgic maybe. Can you do it?"

"I don't know." She gazed at him. His lips smiled, but his dark eyes had their familiar serious expression.

"Try."

"Okay." Nikki shrugged, her heart beating in sharp knocks against her breastbone. She felt shy about showing off, but wanted to prove that she, too, had a share of knowledge, no matter how humble. What she had told him was true, she *did* like poetry, liked the way the words sang.

So they passed the glittering Shalimar while Nikki recited "Freedom is a Noble Thing," and the glitz of Vegas World as she gave herself to the eerie rhythms of the ballad of True Thomas and the Elfland Queen.

By the time they reached the Sahara, its towering sign topped by a neon flame, she had started a poem called, simply, "Song." She finished it just as they reached the pink and white building that was home to Circus Circus. The poem was a strange one, in which the hapless narrator was first tempted by a god of love, then trapped in a cage.

Gil stopped again, his face solemn. He kept his arm linked through hers. With his free hand he adjusted her ponytails so that they cascaded down the front of the leather jacket. He fingered one as he might a piece of silk.

"Are all your poems cynical, Nikki? Is that the way you feel?"

She eyed him warily, her lips parted. She hadn't thought the poems cynical. She'd thought only of their beauty. "I don't know what you mean."

He continued to toy with her hair. "There's a pattern to them. Men are deceivers ever, Freedom is a noble thing, True Thomas Kisses the Elf Queen and she takes him prisoner, and when love comes along, it puts you in a cage. Is that how you see love? Life?''

Nikki laughed, trying to avoid the question. She nodded at a statue on one side of them, then at an enormous neon sign on the other. "Don't ask such serious things. We're standing between a gorilla statue and a neon clown about fifty feet tall. And I've never seen a building shaped like a circus tent before.''

"I mean it, Nikki.'' His hands fell to her shoulder, squeezing it to show his question was asked in earnest. Challenge edged his voice.

"I mean it, too,'' she said airily. "This is the strangest place we've seen. It doesn't look like a building. It looks like a big pink and white—confection.''

"Right.'' The line of his mouth was severe. "And you're being a bit of a confection yourself. That aloof and slightly mocking act of yours—the one you use when you want to keep people at a distance.''

She tried not to wince. Instead, she maintained exactly the manner he'd criticized, aloof and slightly mocking. "I won't dissect my personality while I'm standing between a gorilla and a clown. It's all too appropriate. Another time—all right?''

He put both hands on her shoulders. "Another time— soon. I've got three questions for you, Nikki. Two I want answered before the night is over. And I want straight answers. The third can wait until after—until later.''

She gazed at him apprehensively. The neon from the giant clown sign flickered behind him, red and blue, pink and gold. "I don't,'' she said slowly, "have to answer any questions at all.''

"No,'' he answered, squeezing her shoulders. "You don't. And maybe you won't. Maybe you're not brave enough. We'll see. In the meantime, kid—'' he flicked one of her ponytails sardonically "—come on. I'll take you to the circus."

She tossed her head so that her ponytails spilled down her back again. Glancing behind, she saw Moses, loitering by the immense white statue of a clown. He didn't seem to be watching them, but she knew he was alert, keeping guard.

INSIDE CIRCUS CIRCUS Nikki was bombarded by lights and color and movement, by music and noise and the cries of barkers, the scent of popcorn and peanuts. A blue-haired clown face grinned down at her from a spangled carousel. All around her stretched a glittering midway, bright with game booths and prizes.

"Like a county fair with delusions of grandeur," Gil said wryly. "Did you ever go to a county fair? Have your boyfriend show off and win you a stuffed animal?"

Nikki shook her head, hardly knowing where to look. She found herself fascinated by a race of mechanized camels over a mechanized desert.

"Then you must have had an underprivileged childhood," he said.

She looked up sharply, but he was smiling his one-sided smile, only joking, not judging her. "My childhood was perfectly fine," she said tightly, but her hands inside the jacket pockets balled into tense fists.

"Good. But at a carnival, every girl needs a man to win her useless prizes. To have him show off just for her."

Nikki shrugged. "I don't want a man doing anything for me." She threw a discreet look over her shoulder. Moses was a few yards behind them, pretending to watch a group of tourists playing a penny-pitch game.

"Ah, Nikki," Gil said from between his teeth, "you're a hard case. If you won't play the slots, you need to do something. I used to be pretty good with a basketball. Let's see if we can get you one of those stuffed dogs."

Nikki looked down at the floor, embarrassed. "What would I want with a stuffed dog? I'm not a child."

"You can practice hugging it. You don't like practicing with me. At least you don't want to like it."

"Oh, *really,*" she said with a shake of her head. He lay down his money to take a chance at shooting baskets, but she refused to watch. She turned away and stared at a ring toss game. She wished she had stayed in the penthouse.

Her brooding was interrupted when Gil tapped her on the shoulder and thrust an enormous white stuffed dog into her arms. It was almost three feet tall, with thick white fur, black button eyes and a red ribbon around its neck. She took it reluctantly, yet felt a strange pleasure.

"Is that almost a smile I see?" Gil asked, one eyebrow raised. "No? Then I'll have to get you another animal. And maybe another and another."

"*No,*" Nikki protested, "this one's so big I can't see over it."

"Yes," he teased. "You need a matched set."

Nikki watched, with grudging admiration, as he made the shots. He had a born athlete's grace and a sureness of movement, and she was impressed by the concentration that settled over his face. Shot after shot sank through the basket without touching the rim.

In a moment, he was putting another dog in her arms. She smiled in chagrin. "I feel silly."

"Good. Vegas is a place to be silly. Let's see—what else do you need? A parrot or two?"

"Gil!"

He laughed as she struggled to glare at him over the two furry white dogs. "At least a couple of parrots," he said. "And maybe a monkey."

"*Gil!*"

At the ring toss he won her three gaudy plush parrots, a pink one, a green one and a red one. Throwing darts, he won her a blue teddy bear almost as large as the dogs. Pitching baseballs, he added two monkeys, one brown and one gray, to the menagerie.

He had to carry one of the dogs, the teddy bear, two of the parrots and the monkeys. "Wow!" he said, looking up at a giant panda displayed over another ring toss game. "Look at that—he must be six feet tall. Let's go for it. It's bigger than Roach."

"No," Nikki begged. "We can hardly carry what we've got now." She tugged at his sleeve.

"All right," he agreed with a sigh. "But I was just getting my feel back for all this. I like it. Makes me feel like a caveman. Get many animals. Get many animals for woman. Show prowess. I'd beat my chest if I had a free hand."

"Come on," Nikki said, trying to hide her smile. "Let's go back to the hotel."

He shook his head. "First to the Hilton. For a quiet drink. Then back to the hotel."

"We can't walk into the *Hilton* with all these animals," she argued. "It's a fancy place. I'll look like a giant hair ball. So will you."

"Honey, this is Las Vegas," he said. "They've seen stranger sights than walking hair balls. I guarantee it."

Nikki shrugged in resignation, but felt a strange and pleasant shiver at being called "honey." She supposed men from Hollywood called all women "honey" and "sweetheart," and the terms meant nothing.

Outside the night air felt cleanly pleasant after the noise and flash of Circus Circus. The walk to the Hilton was short, and the Hilton, although huge, had a more sedate appearance than many of the hotels Nikki had seen.

They passed through the Hilton's casino with its marble pillars and ornately patterned carpet. Nikki wondered, slightly dazed, how many slot machines were in it. A thousand? And how many lights glowed down from the massive chandeliers? A million?

She was glad when Gil finally led her to a quiet little café with a southwestern motif. She spread out her animals next to her on the seat of the booth. Moses, she noticed, drifted into the café a few moments after they did and sat alone, looking at a racing form.

A waitress came, setting down menus. Nikki stiffened at the sight of them. She pushed hers away without opening it. Even something as simple as a menu was a potential trap for her. "Order for me, will you?" she asked. "I'm too tired even to think."

Gil ordered chicken fajitas for them, a Mexican beer with a slice of lime for himself and a glass of white wine for Nikki. "You don't drink much," he said, narrowing his eyes. "Would you rather have something else?"

"It's fine. Maybe it'll help me to sleep."

He nodded, leaned back against the banquette. He'd taken off his hat, and now he took off his glasses. His face looked harsher without them, tougher. "Does the thought of tomorrow make you nervous?"

She smiled sardonically but didn't meet his eyes. "The wedding? It's pretty bizarre. But I've got everything memorized. I just hope Roach doesn't change anything at the last minute."

The waitress set their drinks down. Gil twisted the lime into his beer, raised his glass, but didn't drink. He looked over the mug's rim at Nikki. "I said I had questions for you," he said, his voice low. "Two I want answered tonight. Do you want to hear them?"

A familiar uneasiness stirred within her. She retreated behind a cool facade, gave him a condescending smile. "Not really. But ask away. Just don't expect any answers."

He pointed his forefinger at her. "There you go again. That haughty, kind of smirky attitude you hide behind. I bet it's always worked, too, hasn't it? Keeps people off balance. You're good at it. You really are. I don't mean that as a compliment."

She stiffened, on guard. She twirled the stem of her wineglass and kept her chin tilted at a disdainful angle.

He sipped his beer, frowning. "You're not comfortable doing this. This whole impersonation thing. You especially don't like those little love scenes we have to play out. They bother you. More than they should. It's just a job, you know."

"It's an acting job," Nikki said stiffly. "I'm not an actress. It's one thing to look like somebody. It's another thing to have to act like—like a lovesick fool."

"I see." He set down the beer glass, crossed his arms and studied her. "All right. But that's not the whole story. Who are you, really? Where's your family? What happened to them?"

Nikki shrugged. "It doesn't matter. I'm alone. It's no big deal. It's no *tragedy*. I get along fine."

"That's not an answer. I said we have to be a team, and we can be a good one. But I need to understand you. So that's my first question. What happened to your family?"

Nikki stared into her wine. She didn't like talking about her childhood, her family. She had grown up too differently from other people. She felt shy, different, even freakish. But she could feel his eyes on her, as if he could strip her secrets away if he watched her closely enough. She set her jaw stubbornly.

"The second thing I want to know," he said slowly, his voice lower than before, "and I want to know it because I feel it every time I take you into my arms—is why it's so damned hard for you to touch, to be touched, to show affection. To accept it."

She shrugged, bit her lower lip and refused to meet his eyes.

He reached across the table, but his finger under her chin and lifted her face so that she had to look at him. "I suppose the real question," he murmured, "is who was the man who hurt you, Nikki? Who was he? What did he do to you? Did he hurt you so badly you're never going to get over it?"

Nikki's heart leaped like a frightened deer. She stared at him in true alarm. She had two deep and terrible secrets. She kept them hidden as best she could.

He had guessed the first, about men. Would he guess the second, the even more shameful one, about reading, as well? Panic spread like a flash fire through her nerves.

CHAPTER NINE

NIKKI had been trying to tightly control her features. For an instant, that control vanished completely.

Her face paled, her lips parted in surprise, and Gil could only describe the look that came into her eyes as *trapped*. He could almost hear the alarm bells going off inside her head.

Then, as suddenly as her wariness appeared, it disappeared. He saw her *forcing* it away. One corner of her mouth turned up as if she was secretly laughing at him.

She had a way of lowering her eyelashes and giving a sidelong stare that signaled she was far above the cares of ordinary mortals. It was a look designed to shake any man except the most confident. It did not shake Gil.

He knew he was right, dammit. She could hide behind her cool smile, her aloof facade for all she was worth. She didn't fool him. He'd hit the truth, and he knew it.

The pit of his stomach contracted in sickness and anger. She was a pretty woman, a delicate woman, a proud woman, but someone in her past had frightened her badly, making her conceal her warmth beneath a thick shell of ice. She was trying to drive him off with her ice now.

"Nobody ever *hurt* me," she said contemptuously. "I don't enjoy throwing myself into your arms, that's all. What's the matter? Does that bother your ego, Mr. Hollywood?"

She was lying, he knew, lying and bluffing. "Dishonesty bothers me, Nikki. My ego's fine, thanks. How's yours? Why are you so afraid?"

She pushed her wine away untasted. "I'm not *afraid*. I just want this job over with. I want to take the money and run. In the meantime, I *don't* have to tell you my life story."

He leaned his elbows on the table, arms folded. He bent nearer to her, his eyes narrowed. "Look," he said from between clenched teeth. "We've got four more *days* of this nonsense. To say nothing—God help me—of the nights. Why in hell did you take this job when you so obviously hate it?"

"I *told* you," she said angrily, "for the money."

Gil was growing angry himself. She pushed his emotions first this way, then that. Just when he decided he pitied her, that she was a kid in need of help, she'd make him so mad he wanted to grab and shake her.

Then, when his desire to shake her was at its strongest, he realized he *really* wanted to kiss her, to make love to her in earnest. To hold her and touch her until the tension in her body turned to passion. To kiss her until the suspicion in her eyes was replaced by dreaminess and yearning. To feel her lips again beneath his own, answering his own desire.

He hated and fought the impulse. He had no need to get involved with Nikki; she was nothing but trouble.

"Look," he said, his voice harsh, "I've got to work with you, but I can't figure you. You can look like the most desirable woman in the world—you can even flaunt it. But if a man touches you, you shake like a rabbit. You—"

"I do *not* shake like a rabbit," Nikki said furiously. "I *don't*. Maybe you're comfortable with this farce. I'm not. I'm not a performer."

"You *are* a performer," he said, clenching his fist. "You work six nights a week at a dive called Mirages—Liveringhouse told me. You can't say you're not."

"I'm not a performer," she repeated. "I don't want to be. I don't have a talented bone in my body. This job is just a way for me to get away from all the—the idiocy. You like this kind of life. I don't. I *hate* it."

He gave a deep, rasping sigh and ran his hand over his cropped hair. Taking a sip of beer, he leaned back against the banquette. He glanced at her again. She was trying with all her might to look superior, but he could have sworn he saw the flash of suppressed tears in her eyes.

At that moment, all he wanted was to stop fighting and take her into his arms. Maybe she could stop pretending then. And so could he. But that, of course, was the whole problem. Everything between them was based on pretence.

"Look," he said wearily. "I'll put it in the bluntest possible terms. I've tried to show you that you can trust me—all right?"

Nikki said nothing. She held her head high, a look of wary suspicion on her face.

"Quite frankly," he said, nodding in frustration, "I'm tired of trying. My job, whether you like it or not, is to look like I'm making love to you. And—again quite frankly—you're *not* an easy woman to make love to. If I scare you, if all men scare you, if you're frigid, just tell me. Get it out in the open. Then we'll deal with it as best we can. Just be honest, for God's sake."

Nikki gritted her teeth. She took a deep breath and picked up the green plush parrot. "I'm not frigid. I'm not scared. I'm *not* abnormal. I'm a perfectly normal person. What am I supposed to do—swoon at your touch? I ought to throw this parrot right at your conceited head."

"That's another thing," Gil snapped. "I don't *care* if you're abnormal. You've got this crazy obsession about being ordinary. You shouldn't—because you're not ordinary, not by a long shot."

"I am," she insisted, flinging down the parrot so hard it bounced on the seat and nearly fell to the floor. "That's all I ever want to be—ordinary. Oh, I wish this was *over*. I'm going back to the hotel. Alone. Moses can follow me. You stay away. Just stay away."

When she tried to rise and make her getaway, Gil stood and grabbed her by the sleeve, forcing her to her seat. "You're not going anywhere," he said. He sat beside her, knocking toy animals to the ground, pinning her in place next to the booth's wall, trapping her.

"Don't you dare manhandle me," she commanded, more furious than before. She edged as far from him as she could. Warning flashed from her eyes. "I can take care of myself. Touch me again, and I'll pick up something and hit you over the head so hard you'll—"

"I bet you could, and I bet you would." He inched nearer, still keeping her prisoner. "Stop acting up, dammit. You're supposed to stay inconspicuous when we're out like this. Or are you determined to blow this part of the job, too? Roach'll never let you leave the room again. Good God, of all the women in the world, why'd he hire you?"

Stung, Nikki pressed herself against the seat, muscles tensed. Although her face was set more stubbornly than before, Gil could see the tears once more welling in her eyes. They made him hate himself, hate her, hate Chandler, hate Caressa, hate Hollywood, hate the world, hate the universe.

"Now sit there," he ordered, pointing at her again, "and *listen.* I've got a lot riding on this charade. So do you. If you can't be professional about it, I'll have to do it for the both of us. Especially when you pride yourself so highly on *not* being a professional. On being such a nice, ordinary person."

Nikki sat straighter, glowering rebelliously. She blinked tears back and jerked her chin higher in defiance. Setting her mouth in a grim line, she said nothing.

Gil glared back. "You don't scare me, Snow Queen. You just cramp my style, that's all. Now, some answers. How'd you end up being an impersonator when you hate the job? You said your family was in show business. Is that it? What about your parents? What happened to them?''

Nikki's nostrils flared. She raised her chin still higher. "They're dead," she said shortly. "They were singers. Or thought they were."

Lord, Gil thought in frustration, she was in a dangerously emotional state, although she was doing her best to pretend that she wasn't. So was he, but he had to find the truth about her. For her sake as well as his, he told himself.

"What do you mean, they thought they were singers? What happened to them?''

Nikki shook her head, her eyes unhappy. "They were part of a—a kind of folk-rock band. It was called the Keepers." She shot him a challenging look. "You've never heard of them, have you? Nobody ever has."

He met her stare with his own controlled one. "No. I haven't."

Nikki took a deep breath. "Well, how do singers always die? Either an overdose or a plane crash, right? They were doing a tour. It was winter. A small plane. In Kansas. It went down. They all died."

He waited for her to go on, trying to understand what she felt. The only emotion she showed was defiance. "That's it," she said with finality. "Are you satisfied?"

"How old were you?"

"Four." She looked suddenly tired, overwhelmed by memories. He knew if he pushed her now, he could get at least part of the truth.

"Where'd you go? What happened to you?" he demanded.

Nikki shrugged. One of her ponytails had come unfastened. She undid the other and swept her hair straight back, fastening it with one clip. She pulled it so tightly that she looked almost severe.

"My grandmother took me. My mother's mother. For a while. In Hollywood. She didn't like having a grandchild around. It made her feel *old*. She thought herself a movie star."

"Was she?" Gil prodded. "Was she really in movies?"

"Oh, I don't *know*," Nikki said, obviously fatigued and frustrated. "She'd had a few bit parts. Mostly she worked as a bar waitress or collected unemployment. I didn't fit with the image she had of herself, that's all. And we didn't get along. She thought I was—too much trouble."

Gil studied her, his face solemn. He wanted to reach out and loosen her hair from its strict bonds, see it spill free. He clenched his fist more tightly and did nothing. "Then what? Where'd you go then?" he persisted. He kept the iron edge to his voice.

She shrugged moodily, looking at the table. "My aunt took me. My father's older sister. She was a singer, too. Or tried to be."

"All right," he said. "I get the picture. Success didn't exactly run in the family." He unclenched his fist, then tightened it again.

She didn't look at him. She picked up the foolish plush parrot and stared into its unseeing black eyes. "It wasn't that she didn't have talent," she said, shaking her head. "I don't want to be unkind. Or unfair. It's just the breaks never went her way. And she kept getting mixed up with the wrong people."

She stroked the parrot's plush head gently, hesitantly, as if afraid it might suddenly come to life and bite.

He put his arm on the seat's back, almost touching her, but not quite. "By the wrong people, you mean the wrong men."

She nodded and kept stroking the parrot. "Yes. The wrong men."

"And you saw it all," he said, studying her profile. It was such a pretty profile, and he hated the sadness in it.

"Yes. I saw it all. I guess she was one of those women they call male dependent. She just kept getting involved with—these men. None of them were much good."

"And some were abusive." He stated it quietly, as a fact, not a question.

She kept staring at the parrot, tracing her finger along its satin beak. "Yes." She looked as if she did not want to remember because it hurt too much.

"And some of them—" The iron had left his voice, and he felt an unexpected knot in his throat, the kind he hadn't experienced since Melly died. "Some of them tried things with you. Didn't they?"

"They tried." She lifted her face and met his eyes. "When I started growing up. But I never let them *do* anything. I fought." She gritted her teeth and set her jaw. "I got threatened. I got hit a few times," she said, bitterness in her eyes. "But I never gave in. I never let anybody *do* anything to me."

He nodded, wishing the knot would go away. "Yeah. I know you're a fighter. What about your aunt?"

Nikki looked away again. She twirled the stem of her glass and stared at the untouched wine. "Rhonda? She got sick. She lost her voice. She had to go to work as an impersonator, lip-synching to records. At the club. Mirages. The owner—one of the owners, Evelyn, kind of took us in. She's like a second cousin or something. She'd known Rhonda and my dad when they were little."

"And then?" Gil urged. He wished she'd turn and look at him again. Paradoxically, he was glad she didn't. She'd make him do the thing she least wanted, to touch her and touch her and keep touching her.

Nikki swallowed and kept toying with the wineglass. "Then Rhonda got sicker, and Evelyn let me take over her job. I wasn't quite old enough, but Evelyn covered for me. There were a lot of doctors' bills for a while. And then—Rhonda died. There were—other bills. I got everything paid off. And now—''

Nikki bit her lip and squared her shoulders. "And now—when I go back—I'll get out of that club. Evelyn wants to sell her share anyway. I'll get a cosmetology license, and I'll have a—a real *career,* you know? It'll be a *profession.* With security and everything."

"I see." He nodded. "That's why you want to be—just ordinary."

"Yes." She picked up the parrot again and began to stroke it in the same hesitant, absent manner. "See, I didn't exactly have an average childhood. We moved all the time. Rhonda went from job to job. The Catskills. Miami. Boston. Shows, summer stock. That's not for me. I want to stay in one place. Put down roots."

He reached for his beer and took a long pull. "That's exactly what I *didn't* want," he said with false casualness. "To stay in one place. Or have roots. I couldn't wait to get out of Monterey. See the world. Have adventures. Be in the movies and play all day."

Nikki cocked her head and tried to look philosophical. She shrugged. "To each his own."

"Yeah," Gil said. He took another drink of beer. "To each his own." He set down the mug. "My parents thought I was crazy. They wanted me to be a professor. Like my brother." He gave a snort of derision.

Nikki still didn't look at him. "I guess we couldn't be more different, could we? You and I?"

"No," he said. "We couldn't."

They were quiet a moment. The silence seemed to wedge itself between them, an awkward third party, taking over the conversation and ending it.

"Look," Nikki said, setting the parrot down on the table. "I'm not really hungry. Do you suppose you could cancel my order?"

He nodded. "Yeah. Me, either. I suppose we should get back. I'll take you."

They gathered up their collection of stuffed animals. Gil put his glasses on. He got up, threw a twenty-dollar bill on the table and took Nikki's arm when she rose. She started to draw away.

"Listen," he said earnestly, leaning down so he could look into her troubled eyes, "when I touch you like this, it isn't a threat. Understand? It's just politeness. It means nothing. You don't have to flinch. It's just—custom. That's all."

She shrugged, her arm tense against his. "Fine," she said. "I don't want it to mean anything."

He frowned, took a deep breath. "And when I touch you back at the other place, the penthouse, that means nothing, either. It's just our job. Don't get uptight about it."

She nodded, her face frozen, blank, aloof.

He squeezed her arm tighter. "Even earlier tonight," he said, his voice low, "in the shadows. When I kissed you and had you kiss me back. There wasn't anything, either. It was just to get in the mood. It didn't mean a thing. Whenever I touch you, remember that. It doesn't mean a thing."

She nodded more stiffly than before. Out of the corner of her eye, she saw Moses signal for his bill so that he could follow them.

She and Gil left the restaurant arm in arm, carrying their heap of stuffed animals. Nikki thought the two of them probably looked like lovers ending a night on the town.

But inwardly she was repeating what Gil had just said. When they touched, even when they kissed, it meant nothing. Nothing at all.

GIL SAW A PAIR OF CABS near the entrance of the Hilton and hailed the first. He waited until he saw Moses flag the second, then told the driver to take them to the Xanadu.

Gil put his arm along the back of the seat, as he had in the café. And, as in the café, he seemed studiously to avoid touching her. She hugged the huge toy dog she carried more tightly. For some reason, Nikki, who usually avoided touch, found that hugging felt comforting, even heartening.

During the ride, she didn't speak to Gil, nor did he speak to her. Oh, she thought wearily, leaning back against the seat, this had been the most confusing day of her life.

She squeezed her eyes shut in fatigue. For a few foolish moments this evening, she had felt like a schoolgirl with a crush on a handsome and unattainable man. Ashamed, she supposed he had understood all too clearly and had warned her away from such feelings.

Still, he had shown her the city, had insisted on knowing her better. No, she told herself, that was simply so he could work more comfortably with her, that was all. It was because of what he said. She was a hard woman to make love to. He did it for the sake of the work, that was all.

She supposed, tiredly, she should resent him for forcing her to tell him about her past, but she felt only relief, mingled with a strange emptiness.

She wanted to feel close to this man, yet feared doing so. Part of her didn't want to like him, trust him, to admire him in any way. That she did angered and perplexed her.

"Wake up," Gil said in her ear. "We're home."

Home, Nikki thought sardonically. The hotel wasn't a home to her; it was a huge, glittering trap.

"I'm not asleep," she said, opening her eyes, but she had to stifle an involuntary yawn.

"You should be," he muttered. "You're dead on your feet. I should never have taken you out."

"I *wanted* to go out," she argued. "I'd have gone with you or without you."

But she yawned again as they stood on the curb and Gil paid the cabbie. The night was cold, and once more she hugged the big dog to her as she tried to maintain her hold on the rest of the plush animals in her care.

Then, just as Moses's cab pulled around the corner, a man caught Nikki's eye. She snapped to alertness.

The man's hair was hidden by a billed hat. He wore a security guard's uniform, dark pants and a light blue shirt. He was short, almost dumpy, with a pale, undistinguished face—except for his eyes.

Nikki recognized those pallid, icy eyes. It was the same man who had been at the license bureau that afternoon, the one who'd stared after their limousine with the strange smile.

It *was* the same man, she was sure, the one Moses thought might be a potentially dangerous fan. And here he was, dressed as a guard—with a gun at his side.

The man's pale gaze met hers for a fraction of a second, then flicked away with no glimmer of recognition. He melted into the small crowd of people gathered before the hotel entrance, then disappeared inside.

Nikki stared after him, holding her breath, half-fearful, half-fascinated.

"What's the matter?" Gil asked, turning to her as the cab pulled away. She glanced up at him worriedly. Then, furrowing her brow, she looked after the man again, but in vain. Once more, it was as if he had never been there.

"The man with funny eyes," Nikki said in a low voice. "The one at the courthouse—that Moses was worried about. I swear I saw him again. Going into the hotel."

Gil automatically reached for her arm and drew her closer. "Where?"

Nikki, startled by his protectiveness, mentally repeated what he'd told her, that his touch meant nothing. But her heart thudded wildly, whether from his nearness or from the unexpected shock of seeing the man again, she could not say.

"He walked right in the main entrance," she said in a tight voice. "Dressed as a security guard. He—he had a gun and everything."

"*What?*" Gil demanded in disbelief. "Dressed as a guard? He could get almost anywhere in the hotel. You're sure it was the same man?"

She nodded, still watching the door through which he had disappeared. "I have a good memory for—certain things."

"I know." Gil's arm tightened around her.

"It was his eyes," Nikki murmured. "Those almost colorless eyes."

"Look," he said, steering her toward the side of the hotel. "Moses'll be along any minute. We'll wait for him at the basement entrance. We need to check this out."

MOSES GRINNED when he saw them waiting. "You two just about cleaned out Circus Circus," he said, nodding at the stuffed animals. "I thought you'd have to hire a truck."

His smile vanished when he noticed their expressions. His broad, handsome face went somber. "What's wrong?"

Haltingly, Nikki told her story. Moses and Gil exchanged charged glances.

Then Moses studied Nikki, frowning. "You're sure?"

"Almost positive."

"She has a hell of a memory," Gil said. Nikki was conscious of his arm still wound tightly around her. Instinctively she shrank nearer to him as Moses reached into the jacket of his dark suit. She knew his hand was on his gun.

"I'll go up to the penthouse with you," he said grimly. He opened the basement door, looked around its dimly lit vastness, then nodded for them to follow.

Moses ushered them into the elevator. His gun was out now, a snub-nosed automatic. As soon as the elevator doors closed, he reached into another pocket, drew out some sort of miniature walkie-talkie and switched it on.

"Checkpoint Hightop, this is Hercules. I've got Ducky One and Ducky Two in the elevator. We may have a sighting of Gonzo inside the hotel. Repeat, possible sighting of Gonzo *inside* hotel. Dressed as security. I want backup at Duck Pond and a sweep. Over."

An electrified voice crackled something unintelligible to Nikki.

"Affirmative," Moses said. "Over and out." He clicked off the device and put it in his pocket. "I'm dropping you two at Roach's until we check your place—*and* contact hotel security."

His face was so serious that Nikki felt more apprehensive than before. She kept looking at the blue-black gun clenched in his big hand.

"Who's Gonzo?" Gil demanded, drawing Nikki closer. "The guy with pale eyes?"

Moses nodded, but said nothing.

"Look," Gil said from between his teeth, "level with us. Is this guy dangerous? And if he is—how dangerous?"

"We don't know." Moses shook his head. "We just don't know."

"What do you *think?*" Gil demanded. "He's familiar to you people, right?"

Moses shot him a brief but revealing look. "He *could* be dangerous. It's entirely possible. Can you use a gun, De-Spain?"

"Yes."

"Good. I'll get you one."

Moses cast Nikki a troubled glance. Something in it turned her cold. At that moment she knew, with certitude, that if the man called Gonzo proved dangerous, she would be his target.

Moses looked at Gil again. "I'm putting you in charge of her. It's the least conspicuous way. Don't let her out of your sight."

Gil nodded. "It's all right," he said, jaw taut. "I've got her. She'll be safe."

Nikki paled and her heart beat harder. "Look," she protested, "I don't want anybody in *charge* of me. I don't want anybody keeping me in sight."

"Too bad," Moses said without emotion. "Because for the time being, it's like the man says. He's *got* you."

CHAPTER TEN

ROACH'S SUITE was a surprisingly simple pair of rooms on the twelfth floor, just beneath the penthouse. He presided over it like an ill-tempered hobgoblin.

The decor was American southwestern, with earth-tone colors and accents of dusky turquoise. Navaho rugs, paintings with Native American themes and mirrors with frames decorated with the geometric designs of the Plains tribes hung on the walls.

"You've either got very good eyes—or a vivid imagination," Roach grumbled, pacing. "Nuts and loonies, loonies and nuts. They come out of the woodwork when Caressa's around. I spent all those years in law school—for what? To deal with nuts and loonies."

Gil had taken off his glasses and tossed his hat on the coffee table. "What about the Silverado? Have all those rooms facing the penthouse been screened? If a photographer can get us in his sights, so can a sniper."

Nikki flinched when he said it. It had been a possibility she had purposely kept out of her mind.

"Of *course,* they've been screened," Roach snapped. "I told you they'd be. Silverado security is working with us. But if the Xanadu let somebody slip in posing as security I'll slap them with a lawsuit as big as Nevada—bigger."

Gil watched Nikki with disturbing intensity, as if examining her for signs of fear. She crossed her arms, determined to show none.

"I'm calling hotel security again," Roach muttered malevolently. "I'll make their lives living *hell* until this is cleared up." He swore, then stalked to his bedroom to make yet another call. "You two sleep here tonight," he ordered. "I'll take Waldo and Moses's room. I'm putting them in your place." He swore and kicked the door shut behind him.

Nikki, perplexed, turned to Gil. "I don't want to spend the night here with you. This place is too small. There's only one bedroom."

"Spoiled already?" Gil said with a sour smile. He put his hands on his lean hips. "Used to living like a princess?"

"No," Nikki retorted. "I'm used to privacy once in a while, that's all."

"You're supposed to be Caressa. Caressa has no privacy, remember?" He settled onto a couch. He took the gun Moses had given him out of his jacket pocket and examined it.

"Put that away," Nikki ordered. "It's not a toy, and it makes me nervous."

"I know how to use it." He inspected the safety catch, then put the gun into his pocket.

"I don't want you to *have* to use it," Nikki said, turning away. "This is a development I could have done without."

"Me, too." His voice was calm. "But you knew this could happen when you took the job. It goes with the territory."

She crossed her arms more firmly and stared moodily at the wall hanging. She thought it was the sort of Navaho design called a god's eye, meant to keep evil distant. She hoped it worked.

From within the bedroom, she could hear Roach's muffled voice, harassing hotel security. At last he stopped, and an unpleasant quiet descended on the suite.

Nikki bit her lip. She still wore Gil's jacket; she had the eerie sensation she would feel unprotected, vulnerable if she took it off.

"I'll toss a coin with you to see who gets the bedroom," she said, shrugging carelessly. "It's the only fair way."

"We share the bedroom," Gil said. He said it with such finality, such certainty that she whirled to face him.

His expression was stony, his black gaze impassive. "Get the fire out of your eye, Nikki. It's not a proposition. Moses said not to let you out of my sight. He's right—and you know it."

"Well, I'm certainly not going to *sleep* with you," she countered, her cheeks burning.

"Who *asked* you to?" he shot back at her. "There's a couch in there. I'll sleep on it. Somebody could come in either of those windows—in the bedroom, or for that matter, in here." He nodded at the draped picture window.

"Nobody could get in these windows," Nikki scoffed. "He'd have to be a human fly."

"Wrong." He cocked a scornful eyebrow. "*I* could get in. Just rappel down from the penthouse grounds. I know a dozen guys who could do it. Two dozen."

Nikki flung herself down in a blue chair that faced him. That he seemed so calm, collected and rational somehow angered her, but she was determined to seem just as calm and rational herself. "You're a special case," she countered. "You're a stuntman. You make your living doing crazy things."

He ran his hand over his dark hair. "How I make my living isn't the issue. It's whether somebody could get in here. He could. And as a security guard, he could have access to passkeys. We don't know. We have to be prepared."

Nikki tossed her head. "Be prepared. You sound like a Boy Scout."

He gave her a mocking, one-sided smile. "Think of me as a Boy Scout—clean, reverent, helpful, trustworthy."

"Ha," Nikki said uncharitably.

"Don't try to frostbite me. It won't work. We Boy Scouts are ever cheerful, friendly and courteous."

She cast him a baleful glance. "My contract didn't say anything about a man sleeping in my room."

He kept his superior smirk. He shifted his shoulders and spread his arms along the back of the couch. "But who could object to a guardian Boy Scout?" he asked. "Have I told you that I'm also loyal, helpful, brave and thrifty?"

"Then go pitch a tent, Lord Baden-Powell. I repeat, my contract *doesn't* say I have to sleep with a man in the room."

His smile faded slightly but not completely. His gaze became speculative, almost contemplative. "I'll bet you have that contract memorized, don't you? That you know every word of it by heart."

Nikki gripped the arms of her chair and stared at him coolly. "As a matter of fact, I do."

He nodded and smiled again, as if pleased with himself. "I knew it. Well, Nikki, part of our job is to mislead the press. But the rest of it's security. This is a security matter, and Moses is head of security. He says to stay next to you, and I intend to. I also intend to be the perfect gentleman. I wouldn't make love to you if you got down on your knees and begged me."

"Begged you?" Nikki almost sputtered. "Begged you? *That'd* be the day."

His ghost of a smile vanished, and something sparked deep in his dark eyes. "Yes," he returned with a sarcastic nod. "It would, wouldn't it?"

The bedroom door opened and Roach stalked out carrying a sheet of hotel stationery. "I've made some alternative plans for tomorrow in case this matter isn't settled," he growled. He thrust the list at Nikki. "Here. Read this to me. Let me hear how it sounds." He paced to the god's eye hanging on the wall and scowled at it accusingly.

Nikki stiffened in her chair. Carefully, pointedly, she set the list on the coffee table. She eyed Roach coolly. "I'm not your secretary," she said. "Besides, I don't have my glasses."

Roach turned, glaring, but Gil reached across the table and took the list. "I'll read it," he muttered. "I'm not proud."

He took out his reading glasses and put them on. Nikki's heart sacrificed a painful beat. She couldn't help herself. She loved the way he looked in his glasses, smart, in charge of things, almost scholarly. Glasses were supposed to make a man look weaker. They somehow made Gil look stronger, more masculine.

"One," Gil said, reading, "reschedule ceremony. Move it back at least one hour."

Roach nodded. "At *least* an hour. Give security enough time to contend with this."

"Two. If necessary, move ceremony inside from veranda."

"I don't want to do that," Roach grumbled. "I *hate* doing that. Caressa won't like it, either."

"It's safer," Gil said out of the side of his mouth. "It's more sensible. I never understood why celebrities want to have their weddings outside. Not if they want privacy, for God's sake."

"They want to be private in public," Roach sneered. "They want to be secret out in the open. Go on. Finish it."

Gil cocked an eyebrow skeptically. "Three. Hire extra security. Throw cordon around penthouse. Four. Secure twelfth floor, and if necessary, eleventh. Five. Keep principals inside, under highest security. Scuttle all photo plans. Leak gossip."

"I hate cutting the photo plans," Roach complained, and he hit the wall with his fist to prove it. "I *hate* it. That's what this whole masquerade is about, photos. *Damn!*"

"Look on the bright side," Gil said, taking off his glasses. "Maybe we can all go home early."

Something contracted sharply within Nikki. She watched Gil, his glasses in hand, eyeing Roach so coolly. And she realized, suddenly, that when they parted, Gil for one coast, she for the other, she would miss him. She would miss him acutely.

"What about it, Roach?" Gil prodded. "If we're locked up inside, we can't do you any good. What do you say, after the wedding, we drop the whole charade and get on with our lives?"

"*I* decide what needs to be done." Roach frowned and paced toward the bedroom. "I'm moving to the guards' suite. You stay here until further notice. And, DeSpain?"

"Yes?"

"Do exactly as Moses said. Don't let her out of your sight."

Gil put his feet up on the coffee table and his hands behind his head. "Didn't intend to."

"And as for you," Roach said to Nikki, his eyes glittering, "no complaints. If I'd known how sassy you were, I'd never have hired you. So just keep quiet and do as you're told, will you?"

"Yes, *sir,*" Nikki said with the faintest sarcasm lacing her voice.

Roach glared at her momentarily, then turned his gaze, haughty, to Gil. "Take her," he said disdainfully. "She's all yours."

THE GUARD NAMED WALDO brought them a few personal items from the penthouse, but he had obviously thrown them together with little thought.

Nikki, resigned to letting Gil sleep on the couch in the bedroom, looked at the nightgown Waldo had packed. She sighed in despair. "I can't wear *this*. I wouldn't wear this in front of any man." She threw down a naughty confection of see-through lace and gave Gil a worried glance. "And what about you? He didn't bring you any pajamas."

"I don't wear pajamas. Neither, apparently, does Chandler."

She frowned. "Then what do you wear to bed?" She bit her lip and wished she hadn't asked.

"I don't wear anything. Well, maybe a smile."

Nikki snapped shut the valise that Waldo had so hastily packed. She wheeled to face Gil, who lounged on the bedroom sofa, trying to flip cards across the room into a wastebasket. "Don't think for a minute you're going to run around here naked as a jaybird. Don't even talk about it—or I'll sue you. For sexual harassment."

He flipped the three of hearts through the air. It fell into the wastebasket perfectly. "Here? I wouldn't dream of it. You asked, I told you, that's all. But for you, of course, I'll make an exception. I'll sleep in my clothes."

"Fine," Nikki said, throwing back the turquoise-colored coverlet of Roach's bed. "I will, too."

He pitched the ace of spaces, which turned end over end in the air, then landed cleanly in the basket. "Furthermore," Gil said, not bothering to look at her, "I've never sexually harassed anyone in my life. But if I did, you'd be the last person I'd pick on."

"I don't suppose I'm to take that as a compliment."

"Take it anyway you like," he said, and pitched the jack of diamonds squarely into the basket. "Did you understand everything about Roach's alternate plan? Or do you want me to go over it again for you?"

"I've got it down perfectly," Nikki said, her nose slightly in the air. "One, reschedule ceremony. Two, relocate ceremony if necessary—inside. Three, hire extra security. Four, secure twelfth floor. Five, keep us inside, scrap the photo plan, leak gossip."

Gil cocked an eyebrow sardonically. "Impressive. You *do* have quite a memory. What a shame to waste it in Gooseburp, New Jersey."

"Goose*burg*," she corrected, "and it won't be wasted." She marched into the bathroom, closing the door behind her. She loosened her hair and brushed it until it crackled with electricity.

She washed her face, patted it dry, then stared at herself in the mirror. People had told her that she was pretty, but she didn't particularly like her face. It was too delicate. The slightly elfin tilt of the eyes gave it an aloofness she found helpful, but on the whole, the face was too fine-boned for her taste. She would prefer one that showed the determination, the fight within her.

She shook her hair so that it fell around her shoulders in a cascade of streaked gold. She realized, suddenly, that she didn't want Gil to see her bare face again. It always made her feel naked.

Hurriedly she sketched on a severe mouth, applied a touch of eyeliner, made her brows starker. Then she pulled her hair back tightly and pinned it into a twist.

She would, she decided, slip her jeans off after the lights were out. They were skintight, and too uncomfortable for sleeping. The oversize shirt was long enough to cover her decently. It hung nearly to her knees.

Taking a deep breath, she put her hand on the knob and opened the door.

Gil was stretched on the couch, stripped down to his jeans and a white T-shirt. In spite of winter, he was darkened by the sun, and the blazing white of the shirt made his skin seem coppery by contrast.

His arms rippled with muscles, and the hard planes of his chest were clearly outlined. Nikki drew in her breath, overwhelmed by awareness of him.

His dark eyes were trained on her face. "Good Lord," he said in disgust. "You're wearing makeup to *bed*? And why do you have your hair skinned back like that? It's so tight it looks like it hurts."

Nikki touched a hand to her hair. "It's my business how I sleep."

He shrugged one shoulder. "Suit yourself." He'd taken a pillow from the bed and shoved it against the arm of the couch. He lay down, his knees folded so he could fit on the short couch.

"You don't look very comfortable yourself," she said, feeling suddenly guilty. He was far too tall to be at ease on the couch.

He punched the pillow and settled against it, eyeing her with what seemed to be bored curiosity. "I've had worse," he muttered. "When we shot *Hanoi,* I spent a week sleeping in a wet ditch in the Philippines. This is a piece of cake."

Nikki paused, standing by the bed. It was a huge bed, really, larger than king-size, so large she would feel almost lost in it. "I guess," she said hesitantly, "we could share the bed—but only if you'd promise to behave."

"No." He punched the pillow again. "We're both better off with me over here. Don't put temptation in my path. You don't know much about men, do you?"

Nikki's cheeks colored, and she looked away from him. He was right, she didn't know much about men. And if they were in the same bed, it would be far too easy to touch, and once the touching started, where could it end except with them making love?

"Don't tell me you're going to sleep in those jeans," he said, raking his hand through his short hair. "They'll cut off your circulation."

"I'll be fine," Nikki said, drawing back the sheet.

He swore. "Take off the stupid jeans," he said. "Look, that shirt's big enough to cover you like a tent. I'm not going to spring across the room and attack you. Be comfortable, for God's sake. You need your rest. We're got a full day tomorrow.''

Nikki didn't answer, but slipped into bed. Tomorrow she would pretend to become his wife. She lay in bed clutching her pillow.

"Nikki?"

"What?" she asked moodily, squeezing her eyes shut.

"Aren't you even going to shut off the light?"

She clutched the pillow tighter. To tell the truth, she felt safer with the light on. To be alone with him in the darkness seemed too intimate, too dangerous.

But at last she raised herself slightly on one elbow, reached to the bedside table and switched the light off. The room went black. She could hear the sofa creak under Gil's weight.

"Nikki?" His voice was low, slightly gruff.

"Yes?"

"Not all men are bad, you know."

She pulled the crackling smoothness of the sheet more tightly around her. Rhonda had shown a genius for choosing the wrong sort of man, and at the end burned out her hope of love. She had come to fear and dislike men and had passed the feeling on to Nikki. Evelyn's history wasn't much happier. Her husband had been a drinker and undependable. Both women had repeatedly warned Nikki about the dangers of love.

"Nikki?" His voice came across the darkness. "Did you hear me?"

"Yes. I know," she said, wishing she could tune out her intense awareness of him. Not all men were bad, she knew. But all could be dangerous, and Gil was more dangerous to her than most. Wanting him would be purest folly. A man such as he could never return the love of someone like her.

He had been in love with a bright, *educated* woman, one who shared his background of books and reading.

Besides, she had no business falling in love at this stage of her life. None.

But she lay in the darkness, thinking of him, conscious of him, her body aware of the closeness of his. It seemed to take forever for her to fall asleep, and when she did, her dreams were full of him.

As for Gil, he hardly slept at all. Sleeping in the same room as Nikki without touching her was a torture that no man should be forced to suffer. It was a hell of a lot more difficult than trying to sleep in that damned jungle in the Philippines.

He wanted to rise and cross the room. He'd strip those tight jeans off her and loosen her hair so it spilled down, free and soft and ready to be stroked.

He'd kiss the makeup off her mouth and taste her nakedness. He'd hold her in his arms until morning, discovering every delicious inch of her. He'd make her ache with pleasure as he made love to her, and he'd make love to her again and again until they were both exhausted by desire.

He wished to do all these things, but he did none of them. He must let Nikki alone. It was the only sane, the only decent thing to do.

At last, when her steady breathing told him she was asleep, he arose and switched on a lamp. She stirred but didn't awaken. A strand of her severely pulled-back hair had loosened and spilled like dark gold across the whiteness of her pillow. He resisted the urge to touch it and looked away from her, an ache in his groin.

He sat at the small desk in the bedroom, his back to her, and played solitaire until dawn. He wondered how, in the name of all that was holy, he was going to get through another four days of this.

CHAPTER ELEVEN

NIKKI AWOKE to the scent of coffee, bacon and freshly baked biscuits. The drapes were open and brilliant sunshine fell through the window. It was a beautiful, blue-skied morning, and Gil stood in the doorway gripping a tray.

His faded jeans hugged his lean hips and his turquoise blue shirt clung to his shoulders, its color emphasizing his tan. He looked so handsome that it hurt Nikki's heart.

"Hi," he said casually. "It's a nice day. Want to get married? Have breakfast? Not necessarily in that order."

She sat up, desperately smoothing her hair, which had come loose in the night.

"Don't," he said, reaching out and drawing her hand away. "Don't pin it up again. Let it hang free. Can't you be happy just looking natural?"

Nikki tried to blink away the remnants of sleep as she looked at the bronzed hand clasping hers. The warmth and sureness of his touch sent shudders of pleasure pulsing through her. She didn't want such feelings and quickly withdrew her hand from his.

He sat beside her, placing the tray on her lap. He poured coffee from a silver pot, his hand steady. Nikki drew in her breath. She had never had breakfast in bed before. It seemed both wicked and wonderfully nice.

"Everything's going as scheduled," he said, setting the coffeepot on the bedside table. "We get married—" he glanced at his watch "—in about six hours. On the veranda. Security thinks they have everything in hand."

His shoulder brushed hers. She could feel the warmth of his body, smell the faint lime scent of his shaving lotion. She tried to ignore his closeness by concentrating on the food before her. She broke open a biscuit and buttered it.

"The pale-eyed man—they found him?"

Gil watched her as she nibbled the biscuit. "No trace. They hope you were mistaken. But they brought in extra security, just in case."

She set down her coffee cup. Suddenly the morning didn't seem as bright nor breakfast as glamorous. She remembered the man's flaccid face too clearly. "I wasn't mistaken. It *was* the same man. And he was *in* this hotel."

Gil shrugged, his expression somber. He shook his head. "They combed the place. They've added guards at all entrances to the penthouse. Everybody going in and out has to be checked. It's secure."

Nikki set the tray on the table, no longer hungry. She didn't even want her coffee.

"You should eat," he said quietly. "Does it bother you that much? The possibility he might be out there?"

"*All* of this bothers me. I wish it was over." She shook her head, conscious of the tumbled spill of her hair.

"Right." He kept his dark gaze trained on her. "Me, too. A hell of a way to spend Thanksgiving. But—if it helps, I'm here. I told Roach I'd stay close to you. Nobody's going to get near you if I can help it."

His words touched her, but she didn't want them to. She looked away from him. Her face, she realized, must be almost bare, and she wished she had on her makeup. "I *hate* feeling dependent on anybody," she said.

"Don't look at it that way," he said. "We work together, that's all. We depend on each other."

"It's not the same," she mused, watching the pattern the sunshine made on the carpet. "I don't like the feeling that I have to be protected. I can take care of myself."

"But you're not yourself," he pointed out. "You're Caressa. That can be dangerous."

She took a deep breath, then sighed in exasperation. "I'm tired of pretending to be who I'm not. As soon as possible, I'm just going to be myself."

She threw back the covers to get out of bed, but Gil's body blocked her way. "Will you?" he challenged. "Really be yourself? Will you really stop pretending?"

"Yes. Now please let me get up. Or won't you even let me go into the bathroom alone?"

He didn't move. He raised one dark brow wryly. "So you can put on a mask, as usual? Why don't you just stay here and be yourself? Be open and honest, for a change."

"I *am* open and honest," she said. She threw the covers back farther and made her way around him.

"And perfectly ordinary," he taunted.

She stopped and turned to face him. "There's nothing wrong with that," she retorted. "Not everybody needs to live in Hollywood and be in the movies. Not everybody needs to fall off buildings and walk through fire."

He only laughed. "Lord, Nikki, I can't believe you actually slept in those pants. I'm surprised your legs can still move. Your modesty is hardly ordinary. Nothing about you is *ordinary*."

"My pants are no concern of yours. My legs are no concern of yours." She turned from him, aloof. "And I intend to be as ordinary as an old shoe." She strode into the bathroom and clicked the lock shut.

She heard his voice through the door. "As soon as you're ready, we can go upstairs to the penthouse."

Nikki didn't answer. Instead she stared into the mirror, her heart thudding fiercely. Her own face, bare and vulnerable, stared back. "I don't have to *depend* on him," she said fiercely to herself. "I don't have to *depend* on anybody.

Ever. And I *will* be a normal, respectable person—someday."

But his mockery had awakened real fear within her. Perhaps she was deceiving herself, and he was right—there was no way in the world for her to be like other people. Not really. It was a dream as impossible as Rhonda's, as misguided and hopeless.

As soon as Nikki and Gil entered the penthouse, Roach thrust a folded piece of paper into Nikki's hands. "Last minute changes," he snapped. He didn't wait for a reply, but stalked out to the veranda where six florists were decorating a gazebo with flowers and ribbons. The gazebo, all white fretwork, had been assembled only that morning. A fleet of caterers were setting up an enormous silken tent near the lagoon for the reception.

"Now what?" Nikki said worriedly. Gil plucked the paper from her hand and unfolded it. "Nothing major," he said. "He's decided you should wear your hair up. Keep it simple, he says, like the way she wore it in *Video Girl*. After the ceremony, throw the bouquet to the bridesmaid instead of the guests. And don't show your blue garter. Keep it dignified, he says."

Nikki nodded, memorizing the instructions. "That's all?" she asked, relieved.

"That—and when we go inside, I don't carry you over the threshold. We hold hands. Again, we keep it dignified."

Liveringhouse swooped down on them, his forehead gleaming with sweat. "You two stay out of sight—until the ceremony. I don't want anybody to catch on. Get into the bedroom. Hers. I'm using yours—" he jabbed a finger at Gil "—for a message center. Hurry. Shoo! Shoo!"

Seizing Nikki by the arm, he propelled her into the peacock bedroom. Gil followed, a wry smile on his face. "Out of sight! Stay out of sight!" Liveringhouse kept insisting.

"He's hysterical," Nikki said after he left the room. "You'd think *he* was the bride."

"It's all going to be hysterical from this point," Gil said out of the corner of his mouth. "As for me, I could use some sleep on a real bed. Would you mind?" He nodded at the canopied peacock bed.

Nikki flushed slightly, but kept her manner cool. "Help yourself," she said without emotion. "It'll take me a couple of hours just to do my hair. Thank heavens I've got a veil."

"And a bed," Gil said, covering a yawn. He sat down and pulled off his boots. Nikki took a creamy white velour robe from the closet and went into the bathroom to shower and get ready.

When she emerged two hours later, she could hear the rising buzz of voices from the veranda and the penthouse's other rooms. Carpenters banged away in the garden and from overhead she heard the roar of one helicopter, possibly more. She knew that press helicopters were expected and that at least two security helicopters would be in the air, as well.

But Gil DeSpain, shirtless now, slept soundly in her bed, the blue-green silk coverlet pulled halfway up his naked chest. She watched the even rise and fall of his ribs, remembered touching the fresh scar that crossed them, and an odd, choking sensation rose in her throat.

Noises rattled and roared outside the room, and from somewhere Roach was yelling angrily about wedding cake. Panic mingled with awe surged through Nikki.

What Gil had said was right. From this point on everything would be hysterical. Everything and everyone—except him. Outside the bedroom, the world was going mad. Only Gil, half-naked in her bed, was calm enough to sleep.

THE MEMBERS of the five-piece orchestra, dressed in white jackets and black ties, had taken their places. They sat on a fretwork dais the carpenters had erected beneath the grove of palms just beyond the wedding gazebo.

Nikki stood in the bedroom and swallowed hard. Her dark blond hair was swept up softly and her makeup was perfect; even Roach said so. Because this was supposed to be a solemn occasion, she had kept it more natural, less theatrical.

The dress, she decided, would provide all the theater the press expected. In the closet, it had looked traditional and lovely. But when Nikki put it on, she felt transformed, for the gown was far more splendid than she had realized, so splendid it bordered on magical.

The long sleeves of lace, satin and pearl were flared at the top, so striking they seemed fit for a fairy princess. So did the pearl-encrusted sweep of the satin train. The veil, held in place by a crown of pearls, was designed to emphasize the dramatic lines of the gown.

She wondered what Gil would think when he saw it. He had awakened and been spirited off by Liveringhouse an hour before.

The orchestra had already played its opening pieces. A famous Vegas singer had crooned a song about lifelong love. Its last strains were fading. "The Wedding March" was about to begin.

Nikki knew that at this moment, Gil must be standing in the wedding gazebo, flanked by the nervous Liveringhouse, who was impersonating a groomsman. A pretty but quiet girl, rather empty-eyed, was playing Nikki's bridesmaid. Her name was Loretta, and she was Caressa's cousin.

"I hardly know her," Loretta had said of Caressa. "You can bet she'd never ask me to be in her *real* wedding. But she's payin' me to do this—*and* I keep the dress."

Roach, resplendent in black tie, black trousers and satin-lapeled jacket, would give Nikki away. He looked like a troll in formal wear.

The opening bars of "The Wedding March" rang out, chilling Nikki's blood. "Get ready," Roach warned them. "And act natural. Concentrate on the wedding. Ignore everything else."

Someone from the outside swung open the doors of the bedroom. Nikki's spine felt so brittle she thought it might break. Roach took her arm.

"Let the circus begin," Roach muttered. "And you—" he looked at Nikki coldly "—keep smiling."

Nikki forced her face into a smile, but her knees felt like jelly. Loretta was already making her way down the path to the gazebo. The way was strewn with rose petals of yellow and pink.

Two children, a twin girl and boy, had been imported from somewhere to carry Nikki's train. She thought Roach had said they were some sort of stepniece and nephew of Caressa's and that their parents were among the day's guests.

All the guests were either actors or recruited from Caressa's distant relatives, and all were being paid, Nikki knew. Like her, they had signed contracts pledging secrecy. Half their pay would be held back for five days, to insure that the promises were kept.

The afternoon sky was dazzling blue. The orchestra drowned the splashing of the fountain, but the rumble of overhead helicopters threatened to drown out the orchestra.

The path to the gazebo was lined with pink and yellow blooming rose trees, potted in white jardinieres chased with silver. Arrangements of pink and yellow flowers banked the veranda everywhere.

The gazebo was festooned with hundreds of roses and orchids, ornamented with white and silver bows. Through the insubstantial film of her veil Nikki could see Gil, in white jacket and shirt, black tie and pants, standing next to Liveringhouse.

As Roach slowly marched her forward, she noticed, distractedly, that there seemed to be more swans than usual in the lagoon, and that at least another dozen peacocks had been imported. The racket from the helicopters made the peacocks uneasy and, threatened, they spread their magnificent tails.

Nikki stared at the rose petals in her path. She didn't want to meet Gil's eyes. The expression on his face, when she'd first glimpsed him, seemed solemn, almost stern.

A helicopter tried to sweep low for a photograph, lifting rose petals so they filled the air like pastel snow.

"How many copters are up there?" Nikki asked nervously, forcing herself to keep the smile in place.

"Six," Roach muttered. "Caressa's going to be miffed. Liz Taylor's last wedding drew *seventeen* helicopters."

Seventeen helicopters, Nikki thought in horrified disgust. How did celebrities survive, preyed upon as they were by the press? Was the world crazy?

Roach gave her a discreet poke of his elbow. "Don't smile at the ground. Smile at *him,* dammit. That veil's like cobweb—people can see right through it."

Nikki raised her head but still didn't look at Gil. Instead she stole a glance at the Silverado Hotel across the way. How many photographers and news reporters were spying, snapping photos, taking notes? Her heart shriveled at the thought of so many unseen eyes watching her.

Painful as it was, she kept her smile in place. Then, once more, her gaze met Gil's, and her smile fled.

He stood with Liveringhouse at his right and the minister at his left. His shirt and jacket were snowy white, in contrast to the bronze of his skin and darkness of his hair. Liveringhouse, portly in black jacket and tie, nervously clasped and unclasped his hands before him.

The minister, Nikki knew, was really a justice of the peace flown in from Reno. He was being paid a handsome sum to cooperate and keep quiet. He wore a clerical collar and a pious expression.

But it was Gil who caught and held her attention. His expression was still so serious that she clutched her bouquet more tightly, wondering what was going on behind his stern face, his intent eyes.

Guests, perhaps fifty of them, were seated in silver folding chairs facing the gazebo, but Nikki was barely conscious of them, even when they turned to stare at her.

And then, the next thing she knew, she was within the flower-draped gazebo and the minister was saying, "Who offers this woman to give her hand in marriage?" He'd almost had to shout to be heard over the roar of the circling helicopters.

"I do," Roach said, in the same tone he might have uttered, "And good riddance." He stepped away, leaving her standing beside Gil.

Unexpectedly Gil reached over and took her hand. Her fingers felt icy in contrast to his, and she was grateful for the simple human contact.

To Nikki's whirling mind, the words of the service seemed to evaporate; they did not register on her mind.

Then she heard Gil say, "I do," in a strong voice that carried about the clamor of the helicopters.

The minister's gaze focused on Nikki; she had the vague impression that he asked her if she would love and honor this man beside her all her life.

She nodded, feeling voiceless. Gil squeezed her hand. She felt him gazing at her. *Go ahead,* he seemed to say, *it's almost over.*

"I do," she managed to say. Somewhere a peacock screamed, and another shrieked in answer.

Nikki watched as Gil slipped a band of platinum and diamonds onto her finger. It was lovely, but like everything else about this wedding, she knew it was counterfeit.

Then Loretta was tugging at her sleeve and offering Nikki another platinum ring, a man's. Numbly Nikki took it and slid it over Gil's knuckle and securely onto his finger.

The minister pronounced them husband and wife. Nikki sucked in her breath sharply.

Gil drew the veil back from her face. "Nikki," he said, his voice low and strained, "I've never seen a woman look so lovely."

She started to smile in pleasure and relief at his words, but his mouth was already descending to capture hers.

The passion of his kiss seemed almost real, she thought, her mind dizzied by the sweetly hungry force of his lips.

The scent of roses filled the air, and Gil's touch made Nikki's blood purr in her ears so loudly that she no longer heard the helicopters or screaming peacocks. Her hands rose and fluttered to rest against his jacketed shoulders, delighting in their solidity.

As their touch grew more intimate, Nikki saw silver showers of light against her closed eyelids. Tiny, sparkling rivers of fire began to run through her blood. Only being held by Gil kept her from feeling as if she were trembling, helpless and lost, through space.

"Ahem!" warned Liveringhouse's voice, impatient. Gil drew back slightly, then grinned mischievously at Nikki. Liveringhouse tapped Gil's shoulder with irritable energy. "Could we get this show on the road?" he asked.

Gil smiled a cavalier smile, bent and kissed Nikki again. This time her lips were ready, slightly parted, pliant and eager beneath his.

"Ahem!" Liveringhouse repeated, jabbing Gil more energetically. "The recessional—*if* you please."

Once more Gil drew back. He and Nikki turned toward the spectators and he took her arm securely in his.

The music rose again, trying to sound triumphant over the din of the helicopters. Nikki felt almost weightless, as if she were floating as Gil guided her to the grove of pines where they had kissed the night before.

The florists had carpeted that section of terrace with pink and yellow mums, with the exception of a semicircle of marble. That was where the receiving line was to stand, although Liveringhouse, much to his loss of dignity, had to shoo two peacocks away.

"Gee, that was a *lovely* wedding," Loretta said, wiping a tear from her eye and streaking her makeup. "Except for those damn helicopters." She grimaced at once, then wiped her eye again.

"What's the matter?" Nikki asked in confusion and concern. "Did dust blow in your eye?"

"Naw." Loretta shrugged. "I always cry at weddings. That's all."

Nikki stared at her, openmouthed. Gil laughed and squeezed her waist. "There's only one thing wrong with this wedding. It isn't real." He laughed again as another helicopter swept low, looking for a good shot at the wedding party.

Gil drew Nikki farther into the shelter of the pines. "No, two things are wrong," he said in her ear. "She's right— these helicopters. All right, three things—all these damn peacocks."

Liveringhouse swore and had to chase another peacock off. Entranced by the pearls on Nikki's train, it had stalked up behind her and tried to peck them off.

Then the counterfeit guests lined up to congratulate the counterfeit bride and groom. People went through the motions of shaking Gil's hand and kissing Nikki's cheek. Nikki, keeping a rather desperate smile on her face, pretended to enjoy it.

When the last of the guests had filed by, Roach immediately began to give Nikki orders. "Into the bedroom— pronto—and take off that train. It's detachable. Where are those stupid kids? Have the little yard apes run off on me? I don't want that train dragging. Caressa's got to wear it in her next video."

"Her next video?" Nikki asked in dismay. Roach's words about the children were cruel, and for Caressa to use such a beautiful dress for a rock video seemed sacrilegious.

Roach gave a sour smirk. "Has she ever missed a chance to shock people? She's got a song on her next album, 'White for Virgins.' It'll be sexy as hell. Controversial as hell."

Nikki stared at the cynical little man. "I think that's shameful," she said coldly.

"Think what you want," Roach retorted. "She's the millionairess. You're only the hired help. Now *where* are those brats?"

"The boy ran off to be with his parents, Roach." The sharpness of Gil's voice, behind Nikki, startled her. "I've got the little girl. She wouldn't leave until you said she could. Now you've made her cry. Carry the train yourself, you flunky."

Nikki turned to Gil. He held the little girl who'd been a trainbearer. She had her face buried against his shoulder and was sobbing silently.

"Oh!" Nikki exclaimed softly. Instinctively she put out her hand to stroke the little girl's back.

"I don't know what kind of jerk would drag little kids into this circus anyway," Gil said, dark eyes snapping. "She did a good job, too, even with those da—blasted things." He nodded skyward at the circling helicopters. "Then you go and insult her. Apologize—or I swear, once we're out of sight of these cameras, I'll teach you some manners.''

The little girl burrowed more deeply against Gil's shoulder and cried harder. Nikki saw the anger in Gil's face and was frightened. Hastily she stepped between the two men.

"I mean it," Gil almost snarled. "Apologize. And tell her how well she did."

Roach paled, whether with fear or anger, Nikki couldn't tell. But after a moment he smiled his tight smile. "I'm sorry, little girl," he said insincerely. "You did a very good job. You looked very pretty. And as a reward—I'll give you some extra cake.''

Nikki leaned over and spoke in the child's ear. "And I'll give you the biggest stuffed dog you ever saw. One for you—and one for your brother."

Slowly the child stopped crying. She straightened and rubbed the tears from her eyes. She gave Roach a resentful look. From the area of the reception tent, a young woman, obviously the girl's mother, came hurrying.

"See?" Nikki said encouragingly. "Here comes your mama. Everything's going to be fine."

But as she let her eyes rest on Gil, his face still stormy, clutching the child protectively against the white jacket of his tuxedo, she knew things weren't going to be fine at all.

She feared she was falling in love with this man, a man who could never love her in return if he knew the truth about her. She was breaking every rule that Rhonda and Evelyn, in their concern, had drilled into her. But she loved him anyway. She couldn't help herself.

CHAPTER TWELVE

By the time the last guest departed, Nikki's face hurt from smiling. Gil took her by the hand, following Roach's directions, and led her to the doors of the peacock bedroom.

For once, the jeweled grandeur of the bedroom seemed almost homey. Nikki sank onto the silken edge of the canopied bed, sighing shakily. She was so relieved that the wedding ordeal was finished, she felt as if all her bones had turned to liquid.

Nikki took off her veil and lay it on the embroidered satin pillow sham. Then she laughed for no reason at all—except that the ceremony was over.

Gil shouldered his way out of his tuxedo jacket, hung it on the back of a gold chair, loosened his tie and undid the top of his shirt. Then he sat beside her companionably.

"Lord," he said, shaking his head. "Did you ever see such a circus?"

"No," Nikki said, "Even Circus Circus isn't *that* big a circus."

He fell back on the bed with a chuckle. "How about when the peacock sneaked into the tent and bit the minister?"

Nikki smiled. "How about the second time it came in? And pecked the caterer? And made him drop the groom's cake?"

Gil laughed again. "You were supposed to toss the bouquet to the bridesmaid—but she missed it. And it hit Roach on the ear. I can't believe that was an accident."

"It *was*," she insisted. "And remember when that helicopter buzzed so close, we thought the tent was going to cave in on us?"

He shook his head, his grin fading. "That wasn't funny. That was too close. It was dangerous."

Nikki turned and looked at him. Her face went sober. "Sometimes they got so close I was afraid the updraft would suck up the swans. I really was."

He folded his arms behind his head and gave her a one-sided smile. "A peacock got blown into the swimming pool. Waldo pulled it out. Did you see that?"

"I heard about it."

"And Roach made the trainbearer cry," Gil muttered, sobering again. "But you put things right. She loved the dog. She wouldn't let go of it. It was as big as she was."

"I didn't put things right," Nikki objected. "You did. You picked her up *and* made Roach apologize." She gazed fondly at the angular planes of his face.

"I could see she was scared from the start. Those choppers would scare anybody. It was like being under siege. She did great until Roach mouthed off." He shook his head and swore in a low voice.

"But you were the one who noticed," Nikki said softly, ashamed of herself for not having seen immediately that the child was upset.

"He was picking on you about that damned train," Gil muttered. "Besides, you were tense. I'm used to being in front of cameras. You're not. Here, let me help you with that button."

Nikki had been fumbling unconsciously at the back of the gown, groping for the concealed buttons. Loretta, the bridesmaid, had helped her into the complicated gown. She had no idea how to get out of it alone.

"Come down here," he ordered with a soft growl. "I'm resting. Getting married takes a lot out of a man."

His hands settled on her arms and gently he lowered her so that she lay with her back to him. She knew she should object, but was too languid with weariness. She stared at the gold embroidery thread on the pillow sham and felt his deft fingers working against her back.

"Would you really have hit him—Roach?" she asked. His touch, she realized, dispelled the weary lassitude she'd felt, replacing it with tension, an aching tension.

"Hold still," he commanded. "Who makes these things? Elves with teeny fingers? No. I wouldn't have hit him. It wouldn't have been a fair fight. But I might have held him upside down by his heels for a while. To remind him how it feels to be the underdog. Keep still. I've almost got it."

Nikki took a deep, shuddery breath as she felt the cool air of the room kiss her bared spine.

"There," he said softly, undoing the last concealed button.

He drew his finger along her backbone, slowly, sending delicious prickles aching through her system. He eased the edges of the dress farther apart. She felt his breath, warm against her uncovered flesh.

"This fabric's so stiff—cold," he said, touching first the pearl-encrusted lace, then her skin, "but you're soft—warm—silky."

He kissed the sensitive spot between her shoulder blades. "Don't," Nikki said, flinching at the force of yearning that he awakened within her. "Please."

"I meant it," he said, lifting her hair away from her neck and kissing her nape. "You were the most beautiful thing I ever saw. But the dress is like armor. It makes you untouchable. Underneath, you're very touchable. Very."

Nikki sank her fingers deep into the silk coverlet, as if clutching for her self-control. "Stop."

"I can't." He eased the dress open farther still, his hands stroking the bared planes of her shoulder blades.

"I mean it," Nikki said, shutting her eyes and gripping the coverlet harder. "Roach will be here any minute."

"I mean it, too," he murmured, lifting her hair again and nuzzling her neck, "I can't stop. Why'd you lie down beside me if you didn't want this?"

Fired by guilt, she rose on her elbow, jerking away from his touch. "I didn't lie down," she said resentfully, "you pulled me down. Let go—I've *got* to change out of this dress."

She struggled to rise, but he pulled her back to him easily, turning her so that she lay in his arms facing him.

"Say honestly that you don't want this," he challenged, his voice low. "Just say it. And I'll let you go."

One hand gripped her lace and pearl covered elbow. His other arm wound around her waist, and his fingers, warm and hard, spread possessively against her naked back. He held her so closely that each shallow breath she took made her lacy bodice brush against his chest.

He bent and kissed her between her breasts. His hair looked dark as midnight against the iridescent pearls, and his mouth, unlike the pearls' cold hardness, was soft and warm.

She gasped, wanting to push away, but she could not. He raised his head and brushed his lips against hers. "Just tell me to stop, Nikki," he breathed, his mouth against hers, teasing hers, daring her to answer his caresses. "Tell me what to do. Whatever you want me to do—I'll do it."

Nikki closed her eyes and gripped his shoulders. She wanted to thrust him away; she wanted to draw him nearer. His touch made her burn; it made her freeze. Memories flashed through her mind, paining and dizzying her. Her confused desires tore her into warring halves.

"Nikki?"

She could feel his face hovering just above hers, could still feel the tingling warmth of his lips. She wanted to raise her face to his, to taste the magical, drugging power of his kiss again.

But memories and fears tumbled through her mind, and she was as powerless to move toward him as she was to move away. She felt tears pricking at the corners of her eyes, hot, warm and unbidden.

His body tensed against hers. For a long moment he held her without saying anything. When at last he spoke, his voice was harsh. "Nikki—I forgot. Is it really that difficult? Is it that hard to admit you want somebody?"

She said nothing, but turned her face away, trying to hide it against the billowy satin puff of her sleeve.

"No," he said, the same tautness in his tone. "Don't. You'll ruin Caressa's dress. I'm not worth it."

Yes, you are, her mind cried, but she bit her lip and kept silent. He turned her face to his and wiped the tears away. He kissed her again as he pulled her up to a sitting position, but this time the kiss was brief, almost brotherly.

He stood. She opened her eyes but kept them fixed on the bed's shimmering silk. He reached and took her hand.

"Come on," he said, resignation in his voice. "Take off that damned dress and get into something sensible. You're too strung out to think straight—and so am I."

Nikki rose, not wanting to look at him. He released her hand, but put his finger beneath her chin, turning her face up to his. "It wasn't your fault, kid," he said gruffly. "It's been a long day. Go change."

For a moment his hand lingered against her face, and his eyes, dark and unreadable, held hers.

Then he let her go.

WHEN NIKKI CAME OUT of the peacock bathroom, the bedroom was empty, but the door to the sitting room was ajar.

She wore Caressa's designer jeans, black boots and a blue cashmere sweater with golden *C*s embroidered over it. She'd pinned her hair back as severely as she could. Because Gil always said he liked her face best when it was bare, she'd put on more makeup than usual.

She went into the sitting room. Roach sat on the couch. He still wore his white shirt and dark trousers, but his tie was askew. His expression, as usual, was irascible.

Gil stood by the bar, his dark head bent as he poured a bourbon. He looked long, lean and natural in his jeans and a dark green corduroy shirt. Its sleeves were rolled back to expose his sinewy brown forearms.

He glanced up briefly when Nikki entered. He kept his face blank, but the line of his mouth registered displeasure at the artificiality of her appearance. He turned his attention to his drink.

"It was a success," Roach told Nikki without emotion. "We had our own photographer in the Silverado and another in one of the security choppers." He tossed a stack of photographs on the coffee table. "It looks perfect."

Mechanically Nikki picked up the pictures and scanned them. They were freshly developed and glossy with newness.

They were also satisfyingly *bad* pictures. Those taken from the Silverado showed doll-like people with indistinguishable features. One doll figure resembled, most certainly, Caressa. Another, just as certainly, seemed to be Gavin Chandler.

The photos taken from the helicopter were little better. Shot from above the scene, most were slightly blurred and merely showed the tops of heads. Anyone seeing them would think that Caressa and Chandler were the principle figures.

Roach smiled thinly. "*This* is all the tabloids will be able to print. They'll *think* it's Caressa and Chandler. So will the public. It's the hoax of the century."

Nikki set the photos on the coffee table and sat down in one of the chairs. She shrugged, as if barely interested. "Are they married yet? Caressa and Chandler? Did they get away with it with nobody knowing?"

Roach's smile grew more sour and self-satisfied. "That's for me to know. That information is privileged."

"It won't be privileged long," Gil said from the bar. He glanced at Nikki. "Do you want anything?"

"No," she said stiffly. "Thank you."

Gil strolled to the coffee table, drink in hand. He also sat down in one of the ornate chairs. Roach narrowed his eyes.

"What's that mean, it won't be privileged long?" Roach asked, his tone combative.

"Just that," Gil said with easy cynicism. "Too many people know about this farce. Not all of them'll keep quiet. Somebody'll spill to the press. It's inevitable."

Roach glared malevolently. "These people signed contracts. I'll sue the pants off anybody who talks."

"You'd never be able to find out who talked," Gil said. "The tabloids will call it a source or an informant or an insider. Who knows—you might be the insider yourself."

Roach paled with anger. *"What?"* he demanded.

"I've watched Caressa's career," Gil said. "She wouldn't go to all this trouble and expense just for privacy. No—she'll milk this for all it's worth, then turn around and use it for self-promotion. Nobody'll have a chance to leak the truth. You—or somebody else on her staff—will beat everybody to it."

Roach's face wrinkled in disdain. "What do you know— a *stuntman?*" He put a contemptuous flip on the word.

Gil, unfazed, gave him a one-sided, scornful smile. "The tabloids go to press on Friday, tomorrow. By the weekend, they'll be on the trucks, rolling across America. On Monday they'll be on the stands at every grocery store on the continent. Exclusive—Superstars Wed! Photos Inside!"

Nikki looked at him with curiosity. He spoke with perfect confidence, and his words obviously enraged Roach.

"Caressa will be the media queen of the week," Gil said with the same mockery. "But just when everybody's getting bored—say along about next Thursday—she'll have the word leaked. This wasn't the real wedding. There's bigger news still—she and Chandler actually got married someplace else, in perfect privacy. And *that's* the next big story. Somehow she manages to top herself. God, I never saw a woman who could keep herself so dead center in the public eye."

Roach glowered. Two hectic spots of red appeared on his wizened cheeks. Nikki knew Gil had guessed the truth. She could feel it in her bones.

"So what?" Roach asked sarcastically. "If either of *you* talk, I'll tie you up in legal knots so tight you'll wish you were dead. I mean that, dead. We have total control of this story. Total."

"Fine, and welcome to it. But you should let her know." He nodded in Nikki's direction. "Reporters will be camped on her doorstep by this time next week. She has a right to know. And be prepared."

Roach did not so much as glance at Nikki. "All *she* has to know is to keep her mouth shut. If she doesn't—"

"Don't make threats," Gil warned. "Just admit it. We're going to have to deal with the press ourselves next week—right?"

Roach scowled into his drink and for a moment said nothing. "Right," he admitted at last, his tone grudging. "I would have told you at the end, anyway."

Nikki gazed at him in resentment. She'd hoped that everything would be behind her when she flew home. To know the furor would continue, would follow her back, would invade her personal world, angered and sickened her.

Gil shook his head. "You'd have told us to be prepared for reporters and to keep quiet. You wouldn't tell us that you'd be the leak."

Roach shrugged, his mouth set at a sulky angle.

"And Caressa writes this whole caper off as publicity," Gil said derisively. "She deducts it from her taxes. How much did it cost her, anyway? Half a million? More?"

"More," Roach sneered. "She has to have security in two places—here and where she is. Besides—Liz's last wedding cost a million and a half. You think Caressa intends to look *cheap?*"

"No," Gil said, his smile disappearing. "She'd never want to look cheap."

Nikki's heart constricted. Over a million dollars? It seemed an extravagance so huge it was inexcusable.

"What do you care?" Roach challenged. "You're both living like kings. When will you ever live like this again?"

Gil's ironic smile returned. "Never, thanks. I like my own way better. It's saner and safer. Which reminds me—there were a hell of a lot of people running in and out of here today. Is security sure they're all accounted for?"

"Security was excellent. Keepers have to come for the extra peacocks and swans, that's all." Roach's lip curled. "Remind me not to have peacocks next time she gets married. If I ever see another peacock, I'll french fry it."

He rose and straightened his tie. "You two keep a low profile. Go out on the veranda only when I say. We've had good luck. I'm not pushing it any further."

"What about security?" Gil's face was serious again.

"I've reduced security. The wedding was the big target. We're down to the usual. Which reminds me. I want that gun. If you get nervous and shoot somebody, Caressa will end up liable. I sue people. I don't like being sued."

Gil rose, his expression impassive. "I'd rather keep it."

"The emergency," Roach said between his teeth, "is *over*. You want to play cowboy, do it in the movies."

He and Gil glared at each other. Nikki moved restlessly. She was sick of scenes and wanted no more of them. Besides that, the pale-eyed man had never appeared, and the whole episode had been a false alarm. "Give it to him," she said to Gil. "I'm sick of it and everything it stands for."

Gil's gaze flicked to her, studying her.

"Please," Nikki repeated, and she knew her voice vibrated with weariness. "Please. Just get rid of it."

A muscle twitched in his cheek. But at last he nodded. He went to his room, returned and handed the automatic to Roach. "This is against my better judgment," he said.

"I'm the only one whose judgment counts here," Roach said arrogantly. "Remember that."

He turned and left. Gil bolted the door and put the chain lock in place. He turned to Nikki.

"Why do you have your hair skinned back like that? And all that makeup on? Because you know I don't like it?"

She rose and went to the doors to the veranda, turning her back to him. She lifted one of the drapes and stared out. A peacock stared back, fanned its tail proudly and pecked at its reflection in the glass.

"That's it, isn't it?" Gil asked. "You're afraid to be seen without your mask. And you're afraid of being—desired. Or letting yourself desire in return."

Nikki let the drape fall into place. She said nothing.

"You're a desirable woman, Nikki," he said, his voice level. "I mean that as a compliment. A sincere one."

She turned to face him, her expression rigid with control. "Don't bother feeling anything for me—especially that kind of thing. You don't even know me."

She crossed her arms and gave a scoffing little smile. "Of course, you don't *have* to know somebody just to hop in bed with them. I'm not interested in that. Or anything else. Especially with you."

He stood straighter. He, too, crossed his arms, and his chin jutted out militantly. "Especially me? Why? Because I'm part of Hollywood?"

"Partly." As always when he stared at her that way, her heart began to hammer erratically.

"I'll never leave it, either," he said. "It's what I am. It's what I love. It's what I do."

"So be it. Love it. Do it." She shrugged carelessly, as if he was no concern of hers.

"You think your past makes it impossible for you to want a man—let alone love him," Gil said. The muscle in his cheek twitched again. "That's not true. I can tell. It might take time—"

Nikki's face burned. "I don't have time. I'm a busy person. I think this conversation has gone far enough. I think we should stop talking altogether. I'll see you when Roach says I have to see you. Otherwise, leave me alone."

She turned, starting toward her room, fists clenched.

"Or maybe," Gil's voice said, "you're afraid that you're basically not lovable. Not if people knew the truth about you. But I know the truth, Nikki. I think you're desirable—maybe even lovable."

She put her hand on the doorknob, anxious to escape him.

"Nikki!"

His voice rang out so sharply that she paused but kept her back to him.

"I know the truth," he said, voice taut. "I said I had a third question for you. But I won't ask. I'll tell you. You can't read. That's what all the aloofness is about. That's another reason you hide behind a mask. Isn't it?"

Nikki felt as shocked as if she'd been struck. She stood paralyzed, her hand frozen on the knob.

"I knew last night," Gil said relentlessly. "When you looked at the wrong sign. And when I told you to look at the Barbary Coast, I pointed at the Horseshoe. The Barbary Coast isn't even on that street. You didn't know. Because you can't read."

Her shoulders tensed. She knew her cheeks now burned too hotly to face him, so she refused to turn. "I *can* read—some," she said from between her teeth. "I *can*. I'm finishing school, too. I'm almost done."

He'd moved nearer. She could sense him, had a tingling awareness of him. His voice was closer, too close.

"What is it? Some kind of learning disability? Or that your schooling kept getting interrupted? What?"

She whirled to face him. "All right. I'm dyslexic. Nobody knew for a long time. I kept getting yanked from school to school—nobody figured it out. Everybody thought I was stupid. *I* thought I was stupid. I hated school. I quit."

"Nikki, I understand." He reached out to touch her face, but she slapped his hand away.

"You *don't* understand," she said furiously. "Somebody like you can *never* understand. You with your library and your college and your mother who taught and your brother who's a professor."

"I meant—"

"I quit school because all I ever did was fail. You probably never failed at anything in your life. Then, finally, just before my aunt got sick, I found out what was wrong. It was like everything had been dark and then somebody turned a light on. I knew what was wrong and I could finally have hope. I've got a special tutor. I take courses. And I'll get an equivalency degree—that's as good as a high school diploma. Every bit as good. But you don't know how I've had to work for it. Not somebody like *you*."

The corner of his lip jerked, and his dark eyes snapped. "I'm only saying you don't have to dream small. You don't have to end up in New Jersey. It's *not* your only option."

"It's the best option I've ever had," she said, shaking with anger. "And I'm sick of you making fun of it. I've told you and *told* you. I'm going to live an ordinary life."

He caught her by the arms, almost pinning her against the door. "And I've told you. You're not an ordinary woman. You're beautiful. You're intelligent. You've been tempered by fire. And you *want* to feel—you just won't let yourself. Take a chance on feeling. Come back to California with me."

At first Nikki struggled, but now she went still, gazing up at him in disbelief. "What?"

He leaned nearer. "You and I—we're different. But something real happens between us, something strong. Come to California. Chance it. We'll see where it leads."

She frowned. "What are you asking?"

He gripped her more tightly, his face so earnest it half frightened her. "I'm asking you to come live with me. We might make it work, Nikki. It's crazy, but we might."

Her lips parted in astonishment. "Haven't you heard anything I've said? I've got to finish school."

"Finish it in California. You can find a tutor there. The best. I'd see to it."

"*You'd* see to it?" she said, aghast. "I have a job waiting for me. I'm—"

"I'll get you a better one."

"I'm going to be *independent*." Nikki spoke so vehemently it was if she were tearing the words out of herself. "I'll take care of myself. If you think I'm going out to *Hollywood*—to live off some *man*—"

"Somebody's giving you a chance in New Jersey. I can give you a chance in California. What's the difference?" he argued. "Don't have such a closed mind."

She tossed her head and pushed against his chest so hard he winced. She supposed she had hit his cracked rib, but she didn't care. "My mind is not closed—it's made up. There's a difference. And you're just like every other man—if somebody doesn't *give* you what you want, you use force."

He drew back, but his grip stayed unyielding. "I'm not forcing anything. I want you to listen. You've got this obstinate distrust of men—"

"*Look* at you," she said contemptuously, gazing down at his hands. "Why should I trust you?"

"Because you should know by now you can depend on me." Her jerked his jaw up stubbornly, but he let her go.

Her stance was as defiant as his. "I don't want to depend on you. I don't want to lean on you. I don't want to trust you. I have my own plans. I'm not going to traipse off to California to live off you. Get one of your own kind. I don't *want* you."

"Nikki," he said, a dangerous edge to his voice. "I did love another woman once. It's too soon to say what I feel for you—I'll be honest. As for wanting each other—"

She fumbled behind her, clutched the knob and pushed the door open. "I don't want you," she said from between her teeth. "I don't need you. And above all, I *don't* trust you—or any other man. If you want a woman, go find yourself another fool who likes taking chances."

His eyes went cold and he moved toward her. She stepped inside the door and stood her ground, challenging him to come any farther. "Now let me alone," she ordered. "If you touch me again, I'll call Moses and tell him I need protection—from *you*."

They glared at each other. Gil's dark eyes snapped and his nostrils flared. Nikki raised her chin, shook her head in disgust, then took a step back. "Happy wedding night," she said and slammed the door in his face. She drew the bolt to lock him out.

NIKKI FELL ASLEEP out of sheer exhaustion. The day's events had drained her, and her own emotions had worn her out. Not the least of those emotions was guilt. She knew she shouldn't have lain down beside Gil on the bed. She knew she shouldn't have said the things she did.

But then resentment overwhelmed guilt. And then guilt fought its way back, full of fresh strength. Her sleep was filled with uneasy dreams that fragmented and faded into one another with neither pattern nor logic.

Perhaps that was why the hand that touched her face seemed part of yet another dream. At first she thought the hand was Gil's, but then, even drugged with sleep, she realized that was impossible. Gil's hand was strong, lean and hard.

The hand stroking her face was soft, moist and shaking slightly. More disturbing, it had a quality of realness unmatched by any dream.

Confused, disoriented, Nikki turned from its touch, but the hand followed, insistent and unpleasant.

Her eyelids fluttered open reluctantly. The room was dimly lit by a nightlight, and it took a second for her to understand what was happening.

But the hand, plump and damp, stroked her cheek again. Nikki started and gasped as she realized a strange man was sitting on the edge of her bed, bending over her.

She opened her mouth to scream and was terrified when no sound would emerge from her constricted throat.

"You're younger and even more beautiful than I thought," the man almost cooed. He pressed his other hand over her mouth, hard, so that even if she could scream the sound would be stifled.

Nikki's eyes widened in terror. In the shadowy light she could not make out the man's features distinctly. But she could tell one thing—his eyes were inhumanly pale.

"Shh," he soothed, bending nearer. "Don't scream, Caressa. I've wanted you for so long. And I've come for you at last."

CHAPTER THIRTEEN

HORROR SURGED THROUGH Nikki. Instinctively, she bit the man's hand as hard as she could. He cried out in pained surprise, releasing her.

She half-scrambled, half-rolled across the big bed. Leaping out, she grabbed a vase and flung it at his head. The vase missed, shattering against the wall.

This time when she tried to scream, her voice obeyed. "Gil! Moses! Waldo! There's a man in my room!" She threw another vase. It glanced off his shoulder, crashing against the night table.

She snatched up a small table lamp with a metal base and glass shade, brandishing it. The man's shape, a shadow against the other shadows, moved nearer. She saw something in his hand and prayed it wasn't a gun. "Gil!" she cried. "Moses! Waldo!"

She flung herself against the door that led to the sitting room, but it was locked; she had locked it herself. In the darkness and her panic, she feared she could never open it in time.

A shudder of cold air swept over her from the open veranda doors. The drapes billowed, shimmering in the moonlight. When the man moved toward Nikki again, she sprinted toward the doors. For a terrifying moment the blowing drapes entangled her, but she fought her way free.

She ran across the veranda. Although she still wore Caressa's jeans and sweater, she was barefoot, and the icy stones tore at her feet. She headed for the thickest grove of trees, the palms near the waterfall. The chilly night air ripped her lungs.

Nikki resisted crying out again, for fear it would give away her position and the man would hunt her down before help could come. In the shadows of the grove, she stopped, panting. Her eyes strained to see the doors of the bedroom.

The man stood framed in the doorway, outlined by the dim light behind him, staring after her. But then knocking and crashing broke through the night—and the cry of a familiar voice. *Gil!* she thought in panic. He kept calling her name. It sounded as if he was breaking down the door that separated his bedroom from hers.

Gil—don't! she thought, shrinking deeper into the shadows. *I think he has a gun—*

"Nikki?" Gil's voice rang sharp with anger and desperation. "Nikki?"

A splintering sound rent the night air. The sound of a shot rang out, numbing Nikki. A split second later, another shot roared. Her knees sagged, weak. She knew Gil had no gun. Roach had taken it. The madman was armed, but Gil was not. Why had she screamed for him?

The pale-eyed man's form appeared at the doors once more, shadowy against the blowing drapes. He looked around the veranda with an almost dreamy leisure, as if he now could stalk her without worry, without interruption.

He's hurt Gil, Nikki thought. She sank to her knees on the cold stone, feeling sick. What if Gil lay bleeding, needing help? What if he was dead? Dead—no, she couldn't think that. She would not think that.

Then, as if led by some unspeakable radar, the man began moving straight toward the palm grove, where Nikki knelt hidden, holding her breath.

Each beat of her heart seemed to cry out in pain, *Gil! Gil! Gil!* But Gil did not appear.

The man moved nearer. From the lights shining on the waterfall, she could see the strange smile on his face.

Nikki took an aching breath and watched him. Anger and grief overtook her, driving back fear. If the man found her, he wouldn't find her on her knees. She forced herself to rise. She still clutched the small lamp, although the glass shade had shattered. When had that happened? she wondered dully. Her fingers were stained with something dark, as if she had cut herself. She could not remember that, either.

She swallowed. The man moved unerringly toward her hiding place. Had he seen her run there before Gil had tried to save her?

She backed more deeply into the shadows, looking around wildly. Where were the security people? Had no one heard her cries, heard Gil, heard the shots?

The waterfall splashed and hissed, its cascade aglow with spotlights. The swimming pool and the garden statues were also illuminated.

The entire garden, Nikki realized with plummeting heart, was a patchwork of light and shadow—and the light predominated. She must leave the grove if she was to escape—but she could run nowhere without, at least briefly being bathed in light. Wherever she ran, he could see her.

She edged across the stones, chewing her lip. The penthouse, she thought—the penthouse was still dark. She knew her way around it better than he did.

When she'd awakened, she'd panicked, been unable to think or plan. Now she steeled herself, and her mind felt as icy and clean as the stones beneath her feet.

If she got inside and moved quickly enough, she could get to another room, lock him out. Even if she locked him out only briefly, she could use a phone—there were phones in every room, even the bathrooms.

She clenched her fists, swallowed hard. The man moved toward the grove with same dreamlike slowness, the same blank smile on his shadowy face. Inside, too, she thought, steeling herself, were things that could be used as weapons, if she could stay calm enough to use them.

Most important, Gil was inside—and surely he must need her. She must escape, call for help, go to Gil. She had crept to the farthest edge of the grove. Each tree grew from a circular hole cut in the marble, and at the base of each, the earth was covered by ornamental pebbles.

She reached down, seized a handful of stones and threw them, making a rattling, scrambling noise on the grove's other side.

The man, his face half in light and half in shadow, paused, smiled more enigmatically and veered, heading toward the sound. Nikki waited until he had stepped well within the darkness of the trees before she darted out.

She raced toward the opened doors of the bedroom, and when she heard soft footsteps behind her, she ran faster.

"Halt!" a voice thundered across the veranda.

"Hold it!" bawled a second voice.

Moses! Waldo! A wild tide of relief swept through her.

But as swiftly as her happiness rose, it died, for hands seized her roughly from behind, stopping her headlong flight. The man jerked her to him so roughly that she lost her grip on the lamp. It crashed to the stones as he hauled her against him, thrusting his gun against her temple.

Nikki drove her elbow into him and kicked. He grunted with pain but his hold on her tightened, sure and desperate. "Don't," he ordered. "Or I'll shoot. What have I got to lose? If I can't have you, nobody else will, either."

Nikki stiffened, gritting her teeth. The man had seized her perhaps ten feet from the penthouse doors. At the far end of the veranda, she knew Waldo and Moses were crouched, their guns aiming toward the man. But he held her between himself and them, a human shield.

"I've got her," the man called, his voice shrill. "I'm supposed to have her. I'm *supposed* to. I'm the one she sings to. Me. And we're together now. We won't be apart again. Don't try anything. Or I'll kill us both."

Nikki's pulses roared in her temples.

"Where's the man?" She recognized Moses's voice, eerily calm. "Tell us, where is he?"

"Chandler?" The man's tone rose more shrilly. "I shot him. He had no right to her. She's *mine,* dammit."

He's killed Gil. He's killed him. No. No. Nikki's mind clouded, went black, and she almost sank to her knees again. The man gripped her more roughly, yanking her back to consciousness.

Stay alert, she told herself frantically. *He'll make a mistake. He's scared, too. He'll make a mistake, and then I can go to Gil.*

"Let Caressa go," Moses said, in the same slow, steady way. "You can't make it out of this hotel. Security's coming at you from every direction. Give up. Maybe she won't even press charges. Maybe she'll go with you on her own. You don't have to put yourself in danger. Or Caressa."

For a nauseating moment, Nikki felt faint again. The man, maniacal, did not even realize it was not Caressa he held. What would happen when he discovered he'd been tricked? What would he do to her?

"She's *mine,"* he screamed. He jerked the gun away from Nikki and aimed across the veranda, firing three shots. Nikki flinched, half deafened by the blasts.

Suddenly, an earsplitting rebel yell rent the air from above, and a shape hurtled from the roof toward them, flinging itself across the darkness.

The man's body jerked in alarmed surprise, and he tried to raise his gun to fire again. He was too late. The man from the roof crashed down on him, grabbing him by the wrist and dragging him to the stones.

Nikki reeled from the impact, and although she fell, she fell free, knocked back from the struggling men. The pale-eyed man was on his back, fighting savagely, still clutching his gun. The other man, although struggling to wrest the gun away, was clearly overpowering him.

Nikki, the wind knocked from her, tried to think clearly and coldly again. The crazed man had already fired too many times. He must not fire again.

She scurried to the metal lamp base she'd dropped, seizing it. Then she hurled herself toward the man with the gun and brought the lamp down with all her might. He was tossing as he fought, but her blow glanced off his skull. He groaned, his fingers spasmed, and the gun dropped.

She found herself staring across his body into Gil's glittering eyes. Never before had she thought of a man as beautiful, but that was how Gil looked—truly beautiful.

"Thanks," he muttered, his teeth clenched. He hauled the groggy man up by the shirtfront, drew back his fist and struck his jaw. The man fell back against the stones, unconscious, harmless.

Gil rose, breathing hard, reached out and helped Nikki up. For a blessed moment, she thought he was going to embrace her, but he did not. His hands gripped her shoulders, but he kept her at arm's length.

"G-Gil," she stammered, "I heard shots. He said—I thought—he'd shot you."

"He shot *at* me," Gil muttered, his breathing ragged. "Through the door. When I heard the first shot, I hit the floor. He kicked through the door and fired again. I played dead."

"Played dead? Then got up on the roof to jump him?" She wanted to hold him, to be held by him, to feel his closeness, to assure herself that he was really there, really well and whole. But he grasped her shoulders, still holding her

away from him. "How'd you manage?" she asked. "To
fool him—and then make that jump?"

His face was hard in the shadowy light. "I'm a stuntman, dammit. I play dead and jump off roofs all the time.
It's what I do. Are you all right?"

"Yes," she lied. Now that she was safe, fear coursed
through her in sickening aftershocks. Her cut fingers hurt,
and so did her knees; they had been scraped when she'd been
hurled to the stones.

"You look shaky as hell," he said, his mouth drawing
down. "Your hand's bleeding."

"We've got a man down here! Get an ambulance," cried
a voice in the darkness. Nikki recognized it as Waldo's. Her
throat closed, choked by new fear. Moses had been with
Waldo—had he been hit? She gnawed her lip in apprehension.

"Murph! You here?" Gil yelled.

"Yo," answered a voice somewhere behind them. Nikki
turned in confusion.

"Come take the girl," Gil ordered. "Call an ambulance."

"Yo."

Nikki peered harder into the darkness. For the first time
she realized that there were other security men on the roof
besides Waldo and Moses. They, too, must have been unable to fire out of fear of hitting her.

A man she vaguely recognized ran toward her as he thrust
his gun into his shoulder holster. Gil released Nikki with a
motion so abrupt it was almost rough. "Take her," was all
he said. "How bad is it?" he called to Waldo.

"His shoulder," Waldo replied across the shadow-
haunted veranda. "I can't tell how bad."

Gil cast Nikki a cold look. "Get inside and take care of
yourself," he said without emotion. "And next time you
spout off about not trusting men, remember that it was a

man—" he nodded in Moses's direction "—and a damned good one, who took a bullet for you."

Stricken, Nikki watched him stride toward where Moses had fallen in his attempt to save her.

"Come on," said the man named Murph, taking her arm and tugging her toward the penthouse. She didn't move, only stood, staring after Gil, wondering why she'd said all those terrible things to him. Things she could never take back.

"WE'RE SHUTTING this operation down," Roach said, hours later. He paced the gold and white splendor of the sitting room. "We've accomplished both objectives. We kept the press away from the real wedding, and we drew the worst of the loonies out. He won't bother *anybody* any more."

Nikki sat on the couch, still shuddering. The room was full of weary security men in their shirt sleeves and shoulder holsters. Liveringhouse kept drinking coffee, which made him increasingly twitchy. His hands shook when he refilled his cup.

Nikki looked at Roach's thin, scornful face. "That man," she asked, "you *knew* he was dangerous?"

"We *suspected*," Roach said with a hiss.

"What do you mean, he won't bother anybody again?" Nikki persisted anxiously. "We—we didn't kill him, did we?"

She avoided looking at Gil, who stood next to the bar sipping Scotch. He was bruised and scraped, but if the pain bothered him, he didn't show it. His face was grim.

Roach laughed unpleasantly. "You didn't kill him. He's in stable condition. You gave him a headache to remember, that's all."

Nikki sagged back against the couch in relief. She wanted to steal a look at Gil, but did not. He'd been as hard and uncommunicative as iron since the incident. She stared down instead at her bandaged fingers, stinging from cuts from the broken lamp shade.

Moses was in good condition, Roach had said, and would be hospitalized only overnight. His shoulder wound had been a lucky one, more superficial than it had appeared. Nikki was infinitely grateful.

The gold phone rang, and Roach pounced on the receiver. "Yes? Yes? Yes?" he kept repeating with rising irritability. "Yes? Well, then—*you're* liable. There'll be a settlement—in court or out. Take your choice."

He hung up, a satisfied smirk on his face. "That was hotel security. They admit that Ganzer—"

Nikki flinched. Ganzer was the real name of the man who attacked her.

"Ganzer," Roach was saying, "got in last night and hid out in the basement. Tonight, he overpowered the extra caretaker they'd put on to handle the peacocks. They found the guy tied up in a storage closet. Ganzer used the man's electronic pass card and uniform to get to the veranda. Then he jimmied the door. Their lapse, completely." He smiled. "Caressa's probably going to get another million out of this."

Nikki kept staring at her bandaged hand. No matter where Roach started, he always ended up talking about money. She was sick of it.

"Security's been broached once." Roach's voice crackled with efficiency. "We don't want to chance it happening again. We move on. We leak word that Caressa and Chandler have slipped off to Samoa for their honeymoon. We break camp—immediately. The caper's over. You'll all receive full pay."

He'd done it again, Nikki thought moodily—he'd finished on the subject of money. She gave Gil a furtive glance, but as soon as her eyes met his, he turned away.

Oh, don't turn from me, she wanted to cry, but she said nothing and she, too, looked away. *We have to talk. Don't make it harder than it already is.*

Roach consulted his watch. "Caressa's jet is getting ready. All the New York people—we're out of here in an hour. We'll be in Manhattan by dawn. California personnel—" he gave Gil and Liveringhouse a chilly glance "—there's a chartered plane, ready as soon as you are. Get packing."

Liveringhouse seemed startled, and Gil, straightening slightly, looked even grimmer.

"And," Roach snapped, "I *shouldn't* need to remind you all, I hope, that we have the contractual pledge of your silence on this entire event. Any violation will be countered with legal force."

"You're right, Roach," Gil said, his mouth crooked. "Nobody needs to be reminded."

Roach shot him an acid glance. "Why don't you skip the sarcasm, DeSpain? Why don't you go pack?"

"Right," Gil said. "Why not?" His gaze settled, brief and mocking, on Nikki. "So long, kid. Have a good time being an ordinary person in New Jersey."

Nikki's chin jerked, and she sat up more stiffly, hurt and disappointed. *Surely it won't end like this. We won't just fly off in different directions, never saying anything more. Not after all we've been through.*

Her eyes held his for a long, painful moment. Then, once more, he turned away with a nonchalant shrug and left the room. The door shut behind him.

"Come on," Roach said to Nikki. "You and I and Waldo and Murphy are getting out of here now. Somebody else'll pack for us. Let's get going. No more chances."

No, thought Nikki, more dazed and disappointed than before, *it can't be over this fast. It can't.*

But the man named Murphy was helping her to her feet. He took her arm. "Come on," he said softly. "It's over. It's finally over."

"I WANT YOU to think of me as your fairy godmother," said a breathless, slightly affected voice on the phone. It was Caressa. "We've worried about Ganzer for a long time. You helped bring him into the open. I want to reward you. Roach told you, didn't he? I'll give you three wishes—within reason."

It was a week after the break-in and Nikki was backstage at Mirages. Roach had indeed told her such a call might come. She was prepared.

She took a deep breath. Once she might have been too shy to talk to a person as rich and famous as Caressa. Now she had seen what it meant to be rich and famous, and she was not awed.

"Fine," she said, keeping her manner brisk. She was wearing her Caressa costume, and Caressa's hairstyle and makeup. *How odd,* she thought, *that she chose this moment to call.*

"The first wish is the big one," Nikki said, her voice crisp. "A share of this nightclub is for sale. My friend owns it. She needs to get rid of it. I want you to buy it."

There was a long moment of silence. "Nothing shy about you," Caressa said sarcastically. "All right. I'll have my people check it. If it's a fair price, the deal's done. What else?"

Nikki gripped the phone tighter, not believing her luck. She stared at the club's dingy walls. She would be delivered from them at last. More important, so would Evelyn. They both might find sane lives.

"Second," Nikki said, muscles tensing, "I don't ever want my name released to the press concerning this. Ever.

I'm a private person. I want to live—" her voice trembled slightly "—an ordinary life."

Again there was a long pause. "We *want* to tell this story," Caressa said at last. "It's good publicity. It's—"

"It's what *I* want," Nikki said, her determination returning. "You can buy almost anything. Buy someone who'll say she was there instead of me. I told you. I want my privacy, my anonymity."

Caressa sighed as if displeased. "You'd be famous only for a few days. Think of what it might bring. Job offers, for one thing. Lots of them. A known name is a valuable commodity."

"No." Nikki was firm. "I don't want a known name. Anything I get, I want to get on my own."

Caressa sighed again, more lavishly. "You drive a hard bargain, sweetie. But consider it done. Your name disappears from the record. You were never there. Poof—like magic."

Nikki relaxed her grip on the phone. She breathed easy again. She'd got what she wanted. Evelyn would be free of the club, and Nikki was free from the threat of publicity.

"Now," Caressa purred, "what else? Your third wish? Money? Roach underpaid you, you know. I have him *because* he drives such a stingy bargain, but in your case—"

"I don't want extra money," Nikki interrupted. In Caressa's world everything was reduced to a price tag. Nikki didn't want to live that way. "I agreed to work for a certain amount, that's all I'll take."

"Then what do you want?" Caressa cajoled. "A diamond ring? A fur? I hear you looked divine in my white fur. A car? *Not* a house. I'm already buying a club. Remember, I said within reason."

Nikki ran her hand over her crimped hair. "I don't want anything else—except to be myself and be left alone." She paused, a knot forming in her throat. "But you might," she said, her voice tentative, "have somebody tell Gil DeSpain goodbye and good luck. I—I never got the chance."

Caressa laughed. "Roach said you were a strange one. You'd waste a wish to tell somebody hi and good luck? Fine with me. That's all you want to say to him?"

It was Nikki's turn to go silent. At last she said, "Please tell him that I—thank him. With all my heart. I didn't get to—to say that, either."

"Consider it done," said Caressa. "He'll get the message." She said a curt goodbye and hung up.

A WEEK LATER, Nikki received an envelope postmarked Hollywood. She opened it with trembling fingers, not knowing what to expect. It was a note from Gil, printed, very clearly, in bold black letters. Her heart beat hard, and she had to narrow her eyes to concentrate on the words. So many emotions seethed within her that they warred with her ability to process the writing.

But once deciphered, the note was simple. "It was nothing. Goodbye and good luck to you, too. Gil."

Nikki returned the note to its envelope. But she could not bear to throw it away.

"LIFE," EVELYN always said, "has a way of going on." Her share in the club sold, Evelyn moved to Florida and promptly became the co-owner of a bar. After all, she told Nikki over the phone, she missed having nothing to worry about. If she couldn't worry, she said, she'd be bored into her grave.

Nikki, for her part, had found a modest apartment in New Jersey. The one luxury she indulged in was an ornate gold frame for her equivalency degree. She hung the degree on her bedroom wall so it was the first thing she saw every morning when she woke up. She had every word of it memorized.

The six-month training period at the cosmetic shop had sometimes seemed short to Nikki, sometimes long. When she finished the course, she had another certificate to place on her wall. She bought an identical gold frame for it and hung it beside her degree.

For the next six months, Nikki worked hard at her job, fiercely proud of all she had accomplished and especially that she had achieved her goal. She was independent at last. She'd grown confident with the job. She felt proud of *herself*, almost fulfilled.

But something, she knew, was missing. She tried to fit in, to act like any other ordinary citizen of the community, but she felt, somehow, like an imposter.

Gooseburg, she supposed, was no better or worse than any other small town, yet it left her strangely dissatisfied. With a shock, one day, she realized she was *bored*.

Back in the Village, she had yearned for a safe, predictable routine. Now she had it but was not sure she liked it. She missed Evelyn. She missed the other impersonators. Sometimes she even missed the club.

More than anything, she missed Gil and tried not to think of him. Nikki had considerable discipline, but at that task, she failed; she thought of him every day. She kept thinking of him even when the rest of her adventure dimmed in her memory and seemed no more substantial than a dream.

It was impossible, she thought. Surely she had never worn a mink coat and traveled by private jet. She had never slept in the jeweled peacock room or walked through the ornate rooftop garden. She had never worn a bridal gown worth thousands of dollars and had reporters spying on her from helicopters and hotel windows. She had never been the victim of an attempted kidnapping. It was all a distant fantasy, nothing more.

Only one man, Gil DeSpain, seemed solid and real, yet all she had to remember him by were a few stuffed animals and one terse note. That, and a scrapbook of blurry tabloid photos. She had kept the photos, like the note, because she could not bear to throw them away.

She'd dated a few young men, but had never let them get too close to her. She didn't feel like explaining her problems, and at any rate, they didn't interest her. They were, to a man, safe, predictable, ordinary and kind. They taught her, again, that there were men who could be trusted. But she did not find them interesting.

She wondered what Gil was doing, what risks he was taking, what impossible stunts he was planning and if he ever thought of her. She no longer went to the movies and avoided watching them even on television. They made her remember him so sharply it hurt.

One wintry Friday evening, over a year after the strange, dreamlike circus in Las Vegas, Nikki had been left to close the shop. She was preparing to set the alarm system when the tall man walked in.

"I'm sorry," she said, barely glancing over her shoulder, "but we're closed. We—"

She stopped. She stared at his reflection in the mirrored wall before her. Her breath caught in her chest and stuck there.

Gil, she thought, stunned. *Gil.* He looked a bit older, a bit leaner; his tan was darker than the last time she'd seen him, his hair longer. He wore a tan trench coat, and his expression was serious, his dark eyes intent.

She turned slowly to face him. It was really Gil. It really was.

He said nothing, only stared at her. She said nothing, only gazed back, as if caught in some unbreakable hypnotic spell.

At last, after a time that seemed so interminable it almost made her tremble, he spoke. "I see you still pull back your hair. Will you ever let it down?"

"Someday," she said, clenching the corner of the glass makeup counter. Her heart shook her ribs.

"You still keep your real face hidden," he said, a frown line appearing between his brows.

Almost involuntarily Nikki touched her powdered cheek. She still kept a layer of makeup between herself and the world. The makeup kept her from looking like Caressa. But it did not let her look like the person she really was, Nikki.

"Won't you ever let anybody see that lovely face bare?" he asked. A muscle in his jaw twitched slightly.

"Maybe," she said, her eyes holding his.

"I've been checking on you." His mouth was stern. "You got your degree. Are you proud?"

She nodded stiffly. "Yes."

He nodded, too, looking more thoughtful than before. "And you passed your training. You're really working and living here, right where you said. I suppose that makes you proud, too."

She swallowed. "Yes."

He glanced around the shop with grudging appreciation. "Nice place. Do you like everything as much as you thought?"

His eyes fastened on hers again, demanding the truth.

Nikki licked her lips, tasting the lipstick on them. She stood a bit taller and shrugged.

He leaned on the counter, bringing his face closer to hers. "Are you happy? Completely happy?"

She should lie, for pride's sake if nothing else. But pride didn't seem as important as honesty. "No," she answered bluntly.

He leaned a fraction of an inch closer. He brought his hand to her face and he touched it gently, as if she were something fragile that might break or vanish at his touch. "What's it like having a safe, predictable life?"

She blinked and licked her lips again. His fingertips seemed to burn into her skin like magic points of fire. "I— it gets—boring."

He ran his forefinger over her cheekbone, his thumb along the line of her jaw. Her skin tingled at his touch. "And life without show biz," he asked softly. "How's that?"

Nikki's stomach seemed to have turned into a tumultuous cloud that was flying off without her. "Life without show business," she said, her voice slightly choked, "isn't very exciting. I guess—it was in my blood and I didn't know it."

His thumb trailed over her lower lip, making it tremble. "But you're proud to be independent."

"Yes," she said, lifting her chin higher. "I am."

He let his hand drop away, but his gaze lingered on hers. "I'm proud of you, too." He set his teeth together and grimaced slightly. "I came here—partly—to apologize."

She blinked in surprise.

"When I asked you to come out to California with me, it was stupid, shortsighted, selfish. I should have known—you had to do this. You had to do it. To be a whole person. On your own. I tried to rob you of that."

She gripped the counter more tightly. "Yes."

He nodded, his face solemn. "Will you forgive me?"

"Of course. Oh, of course." The words tumbled out; she'd forgiven him long ago. Hadn't he saved her life? And possibly more lives than hers, as well?

"Listen..." She dropped her gaze to her hands on the counter. She still bore a scar from that night on one finger. "I—I hope you're doing well," she said. "I mean, I don't keep up with Hollywood much. I don't read the trade papers—" She shrugged helplessly, then met his eyes again. "You know," she said.

"I know," he said. He shook his head, seeming to search for words. "I've thought of you. Many times."

"I've—thought about you, too."

"You're the only part of the whole crazy thing that seems real," he said, frowning again.

"I know." She swallowed, breathless, her chest tight.

His sigh was harsh. "I was shooting in Amsterdam, Nikki. You know the business. Here one day, someplace clear across the world the next. No stability, in a way."

"In a way." She tried to sound aloof and knew immediately that she'd failed.

"There's a museum in Amsterdam," he said, his voice taut. "In it, there's a Chinese bowl. A beautiful thing. But it was broken, centuries ago. And all those years ago, they'd mended it."

He raised his hand and touched her cheek again, bending so near that his mouth was only inches from hers. "Nikki," he breathed, "they mended it with gold, pure gold. And I looked at it and thought of you. Only of you."

She looked up at him, bewildered yet happy simply because he was there.

He brought his other hand to her face, framing it. "Life might have broken you. It should have broken you. But it didn't. You're mended everywhere with gold. You mended yourself into something so beautiful I can't get you out of my mind. You're beautiful, Nikki, and smart—and gallant. You met every problem fate threw at you with gallantry. You taught me there's more than one kind of courage. I couldn't forget you. I know—I tried. But after Amsterdam I knew. I love you."

Her lips parted as she tried to think of some reply. Tears stung her eyes.

"No tears this time," he said, bending to take her lips.

He kissed her with such passion she felt half-faint with desire. He drew back, took her hand and led her from behind the counter. His arms wound around her. They were hard with muscle, just as she remembered them.

"I asked you wrong, the first time," he said, pulling her closer. "I'll probably ask you wrong this time, too. Nikki, would you ever consider being independent *with* somebody else? Can you believe that if two strong people love each other, it doesn't make them weak? That it can make them even stronger?"

She put her hands on his shoulders, feeling their hardness and strength beneath the coat. "You were right," she said, her voice shaky. "I tried to be ordinary. It was just another mask. I'm—different. I always will be. Reading will always be a problem for me. Doesn't that bother you?"

"Bother me?" he asked gruffly, pulling her against him and kissing the top of her head. "Good grief, Nikki, we'll be different together. Could you stand my kind of life?"

She nuzzled against his chest, conscious that she was ruining her makeup, rubbing it away. Her hair was coming loose, too, but she didn't care, didn't mind.

"I was bred to your kind of life," she said, putting her arms around his neck. "I just didn't know it. Or want to admit it."

He drew back slightly, cupped her face with his hands again and laced his fingers through her tumbling hair. He smiled down at her, his familiar, heart-shaking, half-serious smile. "You'd come to California? Even if it is all tinsel and chance and make-believe?"

She smiled back. "What I feel for you isn't make-believe. It's real. Even when you were away—it just kept getting more real every day."

He kissed her again, and the shop's dozens of mirrors reflected the event. The real Gil kissed the real Nikki. And she kissed him back, too, too happy, too whole, this time, to want to run away.

"Would you consider being a bride again—a genuine one?" he said, his breath warming her mouth. "Without peacocks and helicopters and bodyguards? Do you *think* you could consider it?"

"Oh, I do," Nikki breathed, raising her lips to him again. "I do. I do."

EPILOGUE

HE WAS WORKING on a film set in New England and shot in Vermont. They were married nearby in a small town so snowy and quiet and quaint that Gil joked it looked like a scene for a Christmas card.

But Nikki didn't pick it for its beauty, but rather for its name, which was Forever. She said Forever was exactly the kind of word she hoped would symbolize their marriage, and Gil was touched by her sentiment.

They chose the smallest, oldest church, a little white steepled one on the edge of town, nestled at the foot of a white-flanked mountain and sheltered by a grove of venerable pines.

They were married on a Sunday evening by the church's minister, Reverend Albert Harper, a small, plump man with rosy cheeks and thinning hair. The church, decorated for Christmas, was sweetly redolent of fir boughs and warm candle wax, and bright with crimson poinsettias in every window and banking the altar.

The minister's wife, a little ginger-haired woman he called Mother, stood up with them and smiled when Gil, nervous, temporarily couldn't find Nikki's ring.

It was the smallest, humblest and most private of ceremonies. Outside the snow fell slowly, in large, dreamy flakes, and the evening light was soft on its untouched whiteness.

Nikki wore a cream-colored silk suit and carried a small bouquet of baby pink and white roses. "I do," she said, her eyes shining.

Gil slipped a plain gold band on her finger and bent to kiss her.

The minister and his wife smiled quietly. How nice, they thought, to see two young people interested in doing things the old-fashioned, simple way. They watched Gil and Nikki contentedly, priding themselves that marriages in Forever, although they might be plain, almost homespun, were sound and solid and natural and made to last.

"Forever," Gil whispered against her lips.

"Forever," Nikki answered, then let him turn the word into a kiss.

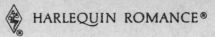

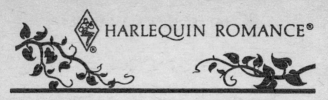

HARLEQUIN ROMANCE®

After her father's heart attack, Stephanie Bloomfield comes
home to Orchard Valley, Oregon, to be with him and with
her sisters.

Orchard Valley

Steffie learns that many things have changed in her
absence—but not her feelings for journalist Charles
Tomaselli. He was the reason she left Orchard Valley. Now,
three years later, will he give her a reason to stay?

"The Orchard Valley trilogy features three delightful, spirited
sisters and a trio of equally fascinating men. The stories are rich
with the romance, warmth of heart and humor readers expect,
and invariably receive, from Debbie Macomber."

—Linda Lael Miller

Don't miss the Orchard Valley trilogy by Debbie Macomber:

VALERIE   Harlequin Romance #3232 (November 1992)
STEPHANIE   Harlequin Romance #3239 (December 1992)
NORAH   Harlequin Romance #3244 (January 1993)

Look for the special cover flash on each book!

Available wherever Harlequin books are sold.   ORC-2